THE GLASTO

There was great excitement in Wessex in 1191 when the monks of Glastonbury Abbey claimed to have uncovered the bodies of Arthur and Guinevere south of the Abbey's Lady Chapel, along with a lead cross which appeared to confirm their identities. It carried a Latin inscription which in English translation reads: "Here lies buried the famous king Arthur in the isle of Avalon".

It was a convenient "discovery" since it made Glastonbury a place of pilgrimage and enabled the monks to refurbish that part of the Abbey which had been damaged by a disastrous fire in 1184. From the offerings of pilgrims who visited the Abbey in great numbers, the monks flourished until the Abbey was closed on the orders of King Henry VIII in the 16th century.

GUINEVERE
AND THE
SIEGE PERILOUS

A Badbury Tale

Philip Elston

MPress books

Guinevere and the Siege Perilous
A Badbury Tale

First published in the United Kingdom in 2011 by MPress Books

MPress Books Limited Reg. No 6379441 is a company registered in Great Britain
www.mpressbooks.co.uk

British Library Cataloguing in Publication Data
A catalogue record for this book is available from the British Library.

Where possible, papers used by MPress Books are natural, recyclable products made from wood grown in sustainable forests. The manufacturing processes conform to the environmental regulations of the country of origin.

ISBN
978-0-9551886-9-5

Typeset in Baskerville
Origination by Core Creative, Yeovil 01935 477453
Printed and bound in England by CPI Anthony Rowe.

This book
is dedicated with
affection and respect
to Her Majesty
Queen Elizabeth II
on the occasion of
The Diamond Jubilee
1952 – 2012

Vivat Regina!

IMPAVIDE REM GERITE

ACKNOWLEDGEMENTS

In developing the characters in *Guinevere and the Siege Perilous*, I am grateful to Susanne in Saxony-Anhalt and Lydia, Monty and Cecilia in Wiltshire for the way in which they brought their "doppelgängers" to life.

I am indebted to the London Eye for being where it is – thereby making an impressive backdrop to the equestrian statue of Britain's 1st century patriot, the Queen Boadicea. She continues to restrain the wonderful bronze horses that carry with them our history and our heritage. Her daughters share with Arthur's mother, Igraine, the degradation of abuse in a male-dominated society. I hope that the story which follows goes some way towards redressing the balance.

The Gloucestershire Police authorities were happy to allow the use of the city of Gloucester police station to appear in the story-line, and BBC Radio Gloucestershire were most helpful in suggesting the Blue Meeting Room as the location for the Sunday evening current affairs programme *Facing the Future*. Sincere thanks are due to my publisher, Andrew Marshall, for his ongoing support and to my wife, Dee, whose labours lap-topped my scribble into readable English.

My final words of appreciation are reserved for Michael, Baron Dobbs, whose generous endorsement of the *Return of the Raven* encouraged me to launch into the writing of *Guinevere* with greater confidence.

Cover Illustration by Tomislav Tikulin.
www.tomtikulin-art.com

AUTHOR'S NOTE

Book one of *The Badbury Tales*, a novel entitled *Return of the Raven*, describes how two teenagers stumble accidentally upon a large underground chamber at Badbury Rings, an Iron Age hill fort in Dorset. Inside, they discover a group of sixth century warriors in deep slumber. Unknown to them they have been followed into the chamber by an elderly man, who rouses the warriors from their long sleep. An inspired adventure ensues; one where chivalry and honour are revived. Although this book is the sequel to the *Raven*, it actually begins six months before the events in book one. In case you wonder what the last two words of the book's title mean, it is an ancient description which in modern language would translate as 'the Dangerous Chair (or Seat)'.

The Arthurian Legend

If Merlin, Guinevere, Morgan le Fay, Launcelot, Galahad, Camelot and The Round Table are stripped away, we are left with a sixth century military figure who displayed outstanding courage and skill. He inspired other men to join him (perhaps as a powerful cavalry force) to drive back the pagan Saxon invaders when the Romans had abandoned the Romano-British population in the previous century. This marked the beginning of the Dark Ages.

Arthur and his men were fighting as patriots and not just for the money paid by local rulers to be protected from the invaders. In twelve decisive battles, Arthur held the Saxons back for some forty years.

In the centuries that followed, many fanciful stories about Arthur were added and brought together by Sir Thomas Malory in *Le Morte d'Arthur*, which he completed in 1470. It was published in 1485 on the first English printing press, introduced by William Caxton.

King
Arthur's
Britain

CALEDONIA

HADRIAN'S WALL

CAMLANN
Camboglanna

YORK
Eboracum

Camulodonum

LINCOLN
Lindum Colonia

River Trent

THE WASH

CHESTER
Deva

BOURNE
River Glen

BRANCASTER
Branodunum

Angles

BURGH CASTLE
Gariannonum

WALTON CASTLE

GLOUCESTER
Glevum

St. ALBANS
Verulanium

BRADWELL
Othona

RECULVER
Regulbium

CIRENCESTER
Corinium

SILCHESTER
Calleva

LONDON
Londinium

RICHBOROUGH
Rutupiae

BAYDON

Saxons

DOVER
Dubris

KINGDOM OF AMBROSIUS

GLASTONBURY

WINCHESTER

PORCHESTER
Portus Adurni

LYMPNE
Lemanis

EXETER
Isca

CHICHESTER
Noviomagus

PEVENSEY
Anderida

ISLE OF
WIGHT

GUINEVERE
AND THE
SIEGE PERILOUS

by

Philip Elston

CONTENTS

Prologue

WHISPERS IN THE DARK

The last Sunday of October was bright and clear as the mid-morning sun touched the Iron Age hill fort; its grass-covered ramparts stirred by a light wind that still carried the warmth of an Indian summer. Soon the peace would be broken by the excited cries of children chasing each other along the steep banks. Meanwhile, the busy hum of half-term holiday traffic eastward-bound was a reminder that from now until Easter every sunny day would be a bonus.

Deep beneath the tree-clad Rings all was cold, dark and quiet as the grave, except for a whisper. Was it a trick of the wind? Or was it a voice speaking to them as they sat unmoving in that hidden chamber beneath Badbury? They sat there in horseshoe formation as if cast in iron or hewn in stone. The whisper returned.

'It will be soon, as the promise foretold. The cold and the dark will be vanquished. Life will warm the flow of blood in your veins and the sun will shine upon your upturned faces once again. Even now the one who will set you free seeks you with relentless determination. Be patient; all will be well!'

The whisper died away but the faintest flicker of an eye lid from the one who sat apart at the mouth of the horseshoe confirmed that the whisper had been heard in the darkness beneath Badbury Rings. However, matters that would play their part in the fullness of time were afoot a hundred miles away, as a raven might fly, to the north-west.

Chapter One
To Sleep, Perchance to Dream

Susanne Jennifer Mortimer's disappearance in the Herefordshire hills on a misty Sunday afternoon in November attracted a lot of attention from the local and national newspapers. She was a strikingly beautiful girl from a well-to-do family and very popular amongst the social group in which she moved.

The police, the army and the local mountain rescue team joined forces to launch a wide-scale search operation over the hilly border country where she had disappeared. But as the hours became days, hope of finding her alive faded and while the local press and radio continued to show interest, at national level the media switched their attention to other more newsworthy stories. Then, five days after she had been reported missing, Susanne Mortimer reappeared.

It was on Friday morning that the police received an anonymous phone call that a young woman answering Susanne Mortimer's description was wandering through one of Gloucester's main shopping malls in an apparently aimless manner. A police sergeant and female colleague were sent by patrol car to bring her back to the city's police station for questioning. As they walked through the shopping mall they spotted her looking through the window at a fashion display in one of the city's main department stores.

'Excuse me, Miss, we have reason to believe that you are Susanne Mortimer and we would like you to accompany us to the police station to help us with our enquiries.'

The young woman looked at the sergeant with a puzzled, almost dazed expression. 'You must be mistaken. My name's Cameliard – Jennifer Cameliard.'

The sergeant was nonplussed for a moment. 'I'm sorry, Miss, but according to our information you answer the description of Susanne Mortimer, who became separated from her family last Sunday afternoon when they were out walking and has been missing ever since. We have a recent photograph of you – of Miss Mortimer – to support the information.'

The sergeant produced a clip-board which displayed a greatly enlarged photograph of Susanne Mortimer. The resemblance between Jennifer Cameliard and the face in the photograph was unmistakeable.

'Would you mind telling us where you live, Miss?' The question was asked in a warm and encouraging tone of voice and Jennifer turned to the police constable.

'That's the strange thing. I don't know – I just don't know. My only recollection is finding myself walking through the shopping centre half an hour ago. I don't know how I came to be here – where are we, by the way?' The sergeant cast a quick glance at his colleague and then decided to take charge of the situation.

'Look, Miss, you've been reported to us as a missing person and you are unable to give us a satisfactory account of who you are or where you have come from. For your own safety I think you should come along with us to the station, where we can arrange for a doctor to check you over. While he is doing so we'll get in touch with your family and let them know that you're safe and ...' He was about to say 'well' but thought better of it in the circumstances. '... we'll tell them that you are safe and sound. Once the doctor's examined you, there's no reason why you shouldn't go home.' He thought she was going to cry.

'Where is my home – to whose family do I belong?'

'Well, Miss, as to that, your father is a Doctor Robert Mortimer and he lives some way out of the city. But it won't take him long to get here and then you'll feel much better. Come along now, Miss, we're holding up the traffic.'

The two women sat in the rear passenger seats and waited while the sergeant called the station to notify them that he was bringing Miss Susanne Mortimer in for a medical check and formal identification by her father.

During the short interval that elapsed between the sergeant moving into the mid-morning traffic and arriving at the Gloucester City police station, a call had been put through to Dr Mortimer at his surgery in Charlton Kings and he asked his secretary to re-arrange his appointments for the rest of the day. As the patrol car pulled into the station forecourt, Robert Mortimer's saloon eased out onto the A40 to join the stream of west-bound traffic moving towards Cheltenham and Gloucester. Twenty-five minutes later, Dr Mortimer managed to find a space in the confined parking area at the police station and hurried into the building. He was escorted to a room off the main corridor and greeted by a woman in her mid-thirties.

'Dr Mortimer? I'm Christine Simpson, the deputy police surgeon. My colleague is down with flu. Do have a seat. I asked the desk sergeant to let me have a word with you before we see your daughter. She's enjoying a cup of coffee with the constable who brought her in.'

'Is she hurt in any way?'

'I can put your mind at rest on that score. I've given her a thorough physical examination and she hasn't got so much as a scratch – just slight exposure. No, the only problem – well, I suppose it's two related problems – is that she appears to be suffering from amnesia ...' Dr Simpson looked straight at Robert Mortimer, '... and she insists that her name is Jennifer Cameliard. No doubt when she is back amongst familiar surroundings the problem will resolve itself. But in the meantime you mustn't be surprised if she regards you as a stranger. I'm sorry.'

'And you say that she has suffered no injury causing some kind of delayed concussion?'

'Not as far as I can tell. Of course you can arrange for Susanne to have a brain scan to see if anything irregular shows up, but all her reflexes are perfectly normal and as I mentioned just now she hasn't a mark on her body. The most obvious factor was the degree of exposure, which isn't surprising at this time of year, but it is fairly mild and a hot bath, a good meal and a sound night's sleep will soon put that right.' Robert Mortimer made as if to stand up. 'I'm grateful to you for taking so much care of my daughter. I'd like to see her now, please.'

'Of course, but can I ask you why your daughter should believe herself to be Jennifer Cameliard?'

The doctor studied his questioner's face for a moment or two, and then nodded as if he had made a decision.

'My wife and I were unable to have any children of our own and contacted a convent near Malmesbury which provided accommodation for unmarried mothers. We never met Susanne's mother – as a matter of fact the sisters did not know who the mother was – Susanne is a foundling. She was abandoned at the gatehouse of the convent when she was only a few hours old. She was wrapped in a baby's shawl which had the initials J.C. embroidered in one corner. My wife has it at home in a chest of drawers. We were never able to trace her mother and after fostering her for some months while the police made the usual enquiries the adoption order went through without any difficulty – Susanne knows all this, of course.'

Christine Simpson nodded. 'There's just one more thing I ought to point out. I don't think it would be a good idea to question her too closely about the past few days. She may volunteer the information in time but I believe the amnesia was triggered by some psychological trauma.'

Robert pondered the diagnosis for a minute or so then looked at Christine. 'I've been a GP for over thirty years but I don't know how to deal with my own daughter who has forgotten her name. What do I call her for goodness' sake?'

'Can I suggest that for the next day or so you don't use her name at all? I'm sure you must have some term of affection.'

Christine stood up. 'Now I think we should go along to see her, then when you are ready you can take her home and give her time to adjust. Here's a week's supply of mild sedatives, although I doubt she'll have much trouble getting to sleep. Meanwhile, if there is anything else I can do, please don't hesitate to give me a call – I've jotted my number on the back of the packet.'

She led the way along the corridor to an interview room. There was a burst of laughter from inside as Christine Simpson tapped on the door and ushered Robert into the room. The constable looked up with a broad grin on her face. 'I've just been telling Jennifer about my Outward Bound training when I was a police cadet. I was supposed to swing across a river and land on the other side, but managed to let go of the rope half a second too soon and landed in the drink instead.'

Robert studied his daughter's face intently, noting how pale and drawn she looked with dark lines of tiredness around her eyes. Biting back his emotion, he went over to her, knelt down by her side and whispered, 'Well, your dear old Dad has come to take you home and let these good people have some lunch.'

His daughter's lower lip began to tremble and he gave her a warm hug, feeling her body tense and then relax as he soothed her and stroked her hair. 'When you're back home Mum will run a nice relaxing bath for you, then you can have a bite to eat before we tuck you up in bed – you can sleep for as long as you like.' He pulled her gently to her feet and then turned to the police constable, 'I don't know your name, but thank you for looking after our darling girl. Maybe next week you might like to come over to our home just east of Charlton Kings to meet my wife and join us for tea.' He gave Christine a warm smile and took her right hand, 'Thank you, Christine, for helping us. We really do appreciate everything you have done – the invitation applies equally to you, of course.'

'Dr Mortimer, the desk sergeant knows I have been looking after your daughter while you have been with Dr Simpson, but if you ask for PC Jackie Wilson, that's me.'

As they were passing reception the duty officer handed Susanne's father a sealed envelope. 'You might like to study the contents when you have a spare moment, sir.' With that, father and daughter left the police station and were soon driving out of the city on their journey home – together. For the first few minutes, neither spoke. 'If you'd rather not talk …' began Robert.

'I do know you're my father, if that's worrying you; I simply don't know who I am any more,' she said in a subdued voice. 'It's as if someone has put a spell on me that made me fall into a deep sleep. When I awoke I was lying in a ditch near the road, except it wasn't a ditch at all but a covered stone chamber like a tomb, although it was by itself and not in a churchyard. I seem to remember that I had no idea where I was when it started to rain last Sunday, and it was getting dark when I spotted it and crawled in to take shelter. Anyway, when I left the shelter this morning I saw a sign-post pointing to a village called Dorstone. I felt very cold and hungry. Thank goodness I had warm outdoor clothing. I set off for Dorstone; it was quite early but light enough to see where I was going and I called at the first house which was showing downstairs lights. A lady answered the door and I told her I was lost and asked her if I could use her telephone – but I couldn't remember any numbers.'

'She took me in, sat me down and gave me a hot, sweet cup of tea, then set about making some cheese sandwiches. I must have looked an absolute wreck. She asked me my name and I told her, "I'm Jennifer Cameliard". She wanted to call the police station at Hay-on-Wye, but I told her I had to get home and that she shouldn't worry. When I'd finished the sandwiches I thanked her and she let me go. I didn't even ask her name.'

She drew a deep breath. 'I started walking and after about ten minutes a milk tanker slowed down – I was on the other side of the road, facing oncoming traffic. The driver asked me if I wanted a lift. It had started to drizzle, so I said, 'Where are you going?' He told me he was going to Gloucester, so I climbed in and he dropped me off near the city centre about an hour later. I didn't really notice the time. He was a very chatty man, which suited me fine. I guess he was glad to have some company. I told him I'd been hill-walking and had a quick breakfast before returning home.' She lapsed into silence.

Robert hesitated before speaking. 'If my memory serves me right, you were about 15 years old when we drove across to Hay-on-Wye for some book festival. We passed quite close to Dorstone and visited a pre-historic burial site by the road side called Arthur's Stone (they call them cromlechs). I remember at the

14

time thinking it would be a useful port in a storm if one wasn't dressed for bad weather.'

A companionable silence settled upon them, which was not broken until they were passing through Charlton Kings. 'We'll soon be home and once we're there just relax and let Mum make a fuss of you. We live quite close to Dowdeswell Court. Years ago, before I set up in general practice, it was used by the Royal Air Force as a conference centre. We have a young family as our nearest neighbours with three delightful children: Lydia is 15, Monty is 13 and Cecilia is 11. They'll be thrilled to have you back - you were their number one baby-sitter and I guess they regard you as an older sister. Since it is Saturday tomorrow, I know they'd love to see you if you feel up to it.'

Robert signalled left and they drove through open white gates along a curved drive flanked by trees which effectively acted as a screen for the large, detached Cotswold stone property. As the car came to a halt, the porch door opened and Sarah Mortimer rushed out to meet them.

'Oh, my darling girl, it is so wonderful to see you!' Her tears of joy and relief were evident to her daughter, who slid out of the passenger seat and was immediately engulfed in her mother's arms. Mother and daughter stood clinging to each other until Robert gently intervened, 'Sarah, sweetheart, how about a nice cup of tea? It does wonders for the soul as well as the body.'

Susanne followed her mother into the kitchen, leaving her father to retreat to his study and open the letter handed to him as he was leaving Gloucester police station; the gist of the letter alerted him to the consequences of his daughter's reunion with her family ... 'You will have been aware of the considerable Press interest following your daughter's disappearance and the publicity given to the search operation. I am sure you will appreciate that her unexpected return home will attract renewed interest and speculation by the media. While we have tried to report the happy outcome in a brief Press release you should be prepared for sections of the local and national media to seek more details. It might be wise, therefore, to issue a personal statement asking the Press and TV to respect your family's privacy while your daughter recovers from her ordeal. In that connection, if you are able to shed any further light on where she was these past few days, I would value access to that information (I have included, as a post script, a secure number that will put you through to me.) Meanwhile, I have arranged for a police officer to patrol the entrance to your property to ensure that news reporters do not pursue you for an 'exclusive' interview. With kind regards, yours etc.'

Dr Mortimer switched on his laptop and wrote a reply to the superintendant's letter, in which he provided a draft appeal for privacy and a detailed summary of his daughter's account of the events she had related on the journey home.

Chapter Two
HOME-COMING

The Mortimers' near neighbours, Douglas and Clare Willoughby and their three children, occupied a spacious barn conversion master-minded by Douglas, a partner in a Cheltenham-based firm of architects. The children had always regarded Susanne as their favourite older 'sister', who was always fun to be around. When she disappeared and the hours became days they were grief-stricken and the Willoughby household, which usually generated joy and laughter, was thrown into gloom and despair.

Clare was driving into Cheltenham for the school pick-up run on Friday afternoon when BBC Radio Gloucestershire interrupted the scheduled programme to report that Susanne Mortimer had been found alive and well earlier in the day and was now back home with her family. It was expected that a more detailed report would be included in the early evening news; meanwhile, Susanne's parents had requested that the media respect their privacy as their daughter needed time to recover from her ordeal.

Clare gave a whoop of joy as the newsflash ended and when her children were in the car and homeward bound, she said, 'Kids, I've some wonderful news! Really marvellous. Susanne's been found safe and well. She's back home again!' The girls were stunned as the impact of their mother's announcement made itself felt and then both burst into tears. 'I thought she was dead,' Lydia cried. 'I did, too,' sobbed Cecilia, 'but daren't say anything in case I made it happen.' Monty remained silent.

'Well, my sweethearts, you won't be able to see her this evening. She's probably exhausted and heading for an early night. After you've had your snack, why don't you sit down together before supper and produce a Welcome Home card? That will mean as much to Susanne as anything else.' Monty broke his silence. 'Mum, where did they find Susanne?'

'There were no details given. If we listen to this evening's local news round-up on TV, we may learn a bit more about it.' Lydia was sitting in the front passenger seat and turned to her mother. 'When do you think we'll be able to see her?'

'That depends on how she feels when she wakes tomorrow morning and what Bob and Sarah think best. If you can get your card finished this evening, you can slip across and pop it through the Mortimers' letter box. You might be invited over sometime tomorrow, but don't get your hopes up too high – and whatever you do, don't start asking Susanne questions, whether it's tomorrow or Sunday. Is that clear?'

'Of course we won't, Mum,' Monty replied. 'I just wondered where Sue has been all this time, that's all.'

'No doubt we'll find out sooner or later,' his mother said with a smile on her face, 'but right now we're also home safe and sound, so let's think about supper and your card.'

When they arrived home, Monty jumped out of the car to open the gate where he was met by the joyous bark and bid for attention by their German Shepherd dog, Caesar, wagging his tail in anticipation of the customary petting by the children before racing off towards the front door as if to say, Now you're home, you can look after the place.

The children piled out of the car and made a bee-line for the kitchen. Monty helped himself to a generous portion of muesli which he drowned in milk, while the girls mashed bananas and covered them with strawberry yoghurt. They made their way to what they called the 'cool room' because it was where they chilled out. Their father's purpose in creating a separate playroom for his growing family when they were younger was to limit the explosion of toys from spreading throughout the rest of the house. There was quiet while they tucked into their re-fuelling snack and gave thought to Susanne's card.

'I think,' said Lydia, 'that we should each write a one-line message and choose what colour we'd like for our own message. How's that for a start?' Her brother and sister nodded approval, then Cecilia piped up, 'What about WE LOVE YOU written in red because Valentine cards are always printed in red or pink?' Monty followed. 'I think WE MISSED YOU should come next.' 'And that leaves WELCOME HOME to round it off,' Lydia responded. 'I like the idea of red as Cee suggested. What colour do you have in mind, Monty?' He hesitated. 'I reckon it should be black, because it was such a miserable time for everyone while Sue was missing.' 'In that case,' Lydia concluded, 'it has to be gold or yellow for WELCOME HOME. Are we all agreed?' She paused. 'Good! Then let's get started.'

Monty interrupted. 'I'm wondering, are we going about this in the right way?'

'How do you mean?' was Lydia's immediate response.

'Well, if we each produce our own part of the card, it means putting separate bits of card on another, larger piece of card and then writing our names underneath. If you ask me, it will look a bit tacky. It would look much better if I create a card on the laptop with colour coded messages as agreed and with our names at the bottom – or simply sign our names in ballpoint.'

'That's not fair!' Cecilia protested, 'I want to do my own.'

Monty shrugged his shoulders, 'What do you think, Lydia? Three bits of card with our own scribble stuck on another piece of white card, or a professional job which can hold its own with all the other cards Sue is sure to get – except that unlike the others, we've all had a part in designing it.'

'Cee,' Lydia looked at her sister, 'I think Monty has a point. At the end of the day it's Sue we're doing it for, and if we send a really attractive card, she'll know that we've all contributed to it.'

Cecilia looked as if she was about to have a big sulk. 'I suppose you're right, but at least let us sign our own names rather than having them printed.'

Agreement had been reached, and they stood behind Monty as he opened the chosen programme on the laptop and began to tap in the contents of the card, with the distinctive messages in their appropriate colours. Once they had all agreed on the design, Monty placed a piece of thin, white card on the feed tray and the printer did the rest. When they saw the result, they realised that Monty had been right.

They went through to the kitchen where Clare was putting together the evening meal. The broad smile on her face as she studied her children's handiwork spoke volumes, but she tut-tutted, 'I am surprised at you all! Not a single kiss to be seen under your names, otherwise it's perfect. Now nip across and post it and come straight back for supper. Dad will be home any time now – but well done, kids. I am sure Sue will love it.'

Two minutes later, their faces flushed with the cold night air, they were laying the table when the phone rang. 'Hi, Clare, Sarah here. What a lovely surprise, and how quick off the mark! Susanne was still awake when I crept upstairs to place it on her bedside table. She cried happy tears and says 'Thank you' to your three lovely angels.' She stopped for a moment and Clare could hear an indistinct conversation, then Sarah began speaking again. 'Sorry about that. Susanne would like the children to come over tomorrow afternoon if that's possible. Bob has to be at the surgery all morning to catch up with today's cancelled appointments.' There was another pause. 'Actually, we'd like you and Douglas to come over as well if you can. There are one or two things Bob and I would value your opinion about. We can use Bob's study while the children have Susanne all to themselves.'

'Of course we'd be happy to come over, and the children will be thrilled.'

'I didn't think you'd mind. You've known Susanne ever since she was a tiny tot. I won't say more now because I know you have your evening meal earlier than we do.'

Clare made no mention of Sarah's call until everyone was settled around the dining room table. She'd phoned Douglas as soon as she and the children had arrived home with news of Susanne's return; now she had more news to share with them.

'I've had a call from Sarah,' she began, 'and we've been invited to go over and see them all tomorrow afternoon, provided, of course, that she has a good night's sleep and feels better in the morning.'

'You know what I said earlier about no questions, but if she wants to talk about what happened, that's up to her, alright?' Cecilia grinned. 'We'll be the first people to see her since she came back. That's awesome!'

During the night the wind veered round and a chill northerly sent the temperature plunging to zero over much of the country and people awoke to a biting cold, frosty morning; a fact that was not lost on the Mortimer family, nor on the small group of photo-journalists gathered at the bottom of the Mortimers' drive where PC Bryan Holden was standing guard.

'Any chance of getting a statement from the family, or better still a picture of Susanne Mortimer, officer?' Bryan Holden turned his attention to the questioner and gave a terse reply.

'You know as well as I do that Dr Mortimer has asked that the media respect the family's right to privacy. The young lady is recovering from a stressful experience, so forget about photo-calls. Why don't you take yourself off and see what Bristol City's chances are in today's match? Now move on and don't even think about trying to sneak in – the law of trespass is still in force, especially if there is harassment involved and a public warning has been given.'

The group dispersed in twos and threes until just one woman remained behind and approached the constable. 'I am sure my colleagues are aware of the situation but you can't blame them for trying. They only want to keep their editors happy. I'm more interested in how she managed to survive and I gather there's a rumour that she's lost her memory.'

PC Holden gave the woman a searching look; in her mid-thirties he guessed. Slim, dark-haired and attractive in a feline kind of way. He spoke slowly,

'Well, Miss, you obviously know more than I do. What paper are you working for?'

'I represent a London-based news syndicate. If I get a story, it's offered to the highest bidder – it's all perfectly legitimate.'

'By which I guess you mean the tabloid press?' She shrugged her shoulders. 'It's a job – I don't suppose I could go far enough up the drive to get a quick shot of the house?'

'That's quite right, Miss, I don't suppose you could, so why don't you join your friends and leave the Mortimers in peace?'

She gave him a sly grin. 'Fine, Officer, but here's my card if you feel able to give me any scraps of information. We pay well and always protect our sources.'

She tucked the card in the pocket of his padded jacket, gave him a mischievous smile, turned and made her way across the road to a black hatch-back, waved and drove away. Bryan Holden fished the card out of his pocket and made a note of her car registration number before studying the details on the card: Morgan Fairchild (Newsworthy Associates Limited, Carmelite Street, London EC4. 'Cheeky minx,' he muttered to himself, 'but pretty with it.' He took his wallet from his inside breast pocket and placed the card alongside a book of second class stamps.

Chapter Three

THE DISCLOSURE

Shortly after half past two on Saturday afternoon the Willoughbys walked across to the Mortimers' house. 'Mum and I saw Susanne last night when you were all in bed. She was wide awake and decided that she'd already slept enough for one week and we were invited to provide company for her. We stayed for just half an hour, I suppose. Both Susanne and her parents were pleased to see us.' Douglas Willoughby stopped short of the house. 'We'll be with Bob and Sarah while you go straight through to the lounge. Sue insisted on getting dressed and she'll be there to see you.'

They rang the doorbell and Bob Mortimer led the children to the lounge door, opened it and popped his head through the doorway. 'Your visitors are here, sweetheart.' Turning round, he gave the trio a broad smile, 'In you go; we'll be having tea with you some time around half past three, I expect.'

'You go first, Lydia,' Monty whispered. 'You're the eldest.' They made a nervous entrance and saw Susanne standing beside a cheerful log fire next to a deep armchair with pillows to give extra support.

'Come along in; don't be shy.' Susanne gave each one of them a big hug. 'It's lovely to see you. Grab an easy chair and make yourselves at home.' They arranged the chairs in a semi-circle around Susanne, sat down, lost for words, and looked around the room as if it were the first time they had seen it. Cee spotted their card, which stood in the centre of a large display from relatives and friends on the mantelshelf above the fireplace. 'We're ever so pleased you liked our card, Sue. We made it as soon as we arrived home from school.'

'It was the nicest welcome home I could have wished for, and I will add it to my little box of treasures.' She went on, 'I wanted to see you all today. Poor Mum and Dad are still in a daze and I am as well, I suppose.'

She settled herself more comfortably in the armchair before continuing. 'You've always been my best buddies, and I need to talk to someone I know well. Mum and Dad are walking on eggshells whenever they are with me, bless their hearts.'

'Mum and Dad said we weren't to ask any questions,' Lydia replied. Then Monty cleared his throat, 'We don't want to upset you or anything …' He tailed off, feeling a bit stupid.

'I understand that,' Susanne smiled at Monty, 'but I need to tell someone other than my parents of what I remember when I was lost …' She paused. 'But I don't want to say anything to you if it is going to be a problem.'

'Mum did tell us that if you had things you wanted to say, that would be alright, didn't she?' said Cecilia, looking at her siblings.

'Your mother is a very thoughtful person, Cecilia, and probably guessed I might have difficulty talking to my own family or total strangers. Are you all up for it, then?' The murmurs of assent were clear-cut.

Susanne relaxed in her chair. 'You know that I wandered away on the hillside last Sunday when it was getting dark – a really stupid thing to do. When it started to rain I began to make my way back to where I though everyone was, calling as I went. They called back but what with the mist and the rain and the approaching darkness, I couldn't make out from

31

which direction their voices were coming. I stood still, calling out every minute, but instead of coming nearer their voices grew fainter until I couldn't hear anything at all.'

She shivered slightly and leaned forward to throw a couple of logs on the fire. The children sat quite still, looking directly at her as she sat back and carried on speaking.

'I realised I needed to get off the hill while there was still a glimmer of light left to see by, or else I might do myself serious injury. Eventually, with a great sigh of relief I reached a road, yet hadn't the faintest idea where I was. To make matters worse, the misty rain had turned into a steady drizzle. I started walking until I came to a road junction, but it was dark and I couldn't read the words on the signpost. I must have been wandering for about an hour and I was tired, thirsty and hungry. I always take a bottle of water and some chocolate when I go hill walking, so I ate the chocolate, hoping a car might come along. Then because chocolate makes you thirsty I drank most of the water. It was then I noticed the stone in the field behind me. It was massive – about two metres in length, a metre wide and perhaps 20 centimetres thick, resting on stone walls either side.'

Susanne smiled at her young friends, whose faces reflected a mixture of fascination and apprehension.

'Shall I go on?'

'Yes please,' Cecilia blurted out, and then blushed when she realised what she had said. 'I'm sorry; I didn't mean I was enjoying it.'

'Well, this is the part which I've not told anyone, and you must promise not to tell. Are you happy about that?' They nodded their agreement. 'I thought at first it was a pigsty, but it was too close to the road and no fence to keep the pigs safe. I scrambled up the bank and crawled inside. I zipped my cagoule up as far as it would go, pulled the hood over my head, curled myself into a tight ball and in no time at all was fast asleep.' She looked at the children and said, 'This is where it gets to be very weird, but before I carry on there's something I need to show you and something I need to tell you.'

She leant across the arm of the chair and took a plastic bag which had been lodged between the chair and the wall. She opened the bag and drew out a baby's white shawl, unfolded it and placed one corner of the shawl on her knees. The children saw embroidered in red cotton thread the letters JC. They looked quite mystified.

Monty was the first to speak. 'Who does it belong to?' 'It's mine, Monty. Mum and Dad adopted me when I was a tiny baby, just a few hours old. I had been abandoned by my natural mother at the convent in Malmesbury, just across the border in Wiltshire 19 years ago. The only clue to my identity is what you see on the shawl.'

The children were even more puzzled. 'What's that got to do with your disappearance?' Lydia asked.

'That's what I'm about to tell you.'

✦   ✦   ✦

While Susanne was sharing her experience with the Willoughby children, Bob and Sarah were unburdening themselves to Douglas and Clare.

'When I drove over to Gloucester to collect Susanne I was in a state of shock, as you can imagine, and on that account I concentrated on getting there in one piece. I left the surgery in a hurry but managed to put a quick call through to let Sarah know that Susanne had been found. On arrival I was met by the deputy police surgeon; a lovely person – Christine Simpson. She sat me down and gave me a second shock. Susanne wouldn't answer to her own name, but insisted she was Jennifer Cameliard – whoever she might be. This is where it gets very quirky. You know that we fostered and then took Susanne for adoption when she was a baby. The nuns at Malmesbury had no idea who the mother was, apart from the fact that she had wrapped the baby in a white shawl with the initials

JC embroidered in one corner.'

'We have always been open about this with Susanne and explained that most probably her natural mother may have been a teenager who became pregnant and somehow managed to conceal the fact, but wanted to leave some hint of her baby's identity when she left it at the convent lodge.'

'I'm sorry to interrupt you, Bob. How did Susanne react?'

'A fair question, Clare, and I think Susanne would agree that because we fed the details over a period of time, as she expressed curiosity as to why she had no brothers or sisters, it didn't seem to faze her one little bit.'

Sarah spoke next. 'Bob's right. We didn't make a big thing of it because she knew that she was safe and secure in the knowledge that we loved her. However, we've no way of knowing what innermost thoughts she may have had and it seemed unwise to intrude in that respect. I think that what's thrown us is that nearly twenty years later, it's come back and bitten us.'

'I'm sure that's not the case,' Douglas interjected. 'In all the years we've known Susanne she has always been open and loving, and clearly appreciates and values your very obvious love for her. She may well wonder from time to time who her birth mother is, and what she is like – that's only to be expected and respected. If she had been nursing any deep resentment or anxiety, you would have picked that up years ago.'

Douglas stroked his chin and chose his words with care. 'It seems to me that whatever prompted Sue to deny her own name is bound up with those missing days. Something quite traumatic must have taken place; until or unless she is able to share that with you, God alone knows whether you will ever discover what actually happened.'

Robert and Sarah looked at one another, then Sarah spoke. 'Bless you, Douglas; you don't know how comforting it is to hear what you have just said. As a matter of fact it confirms exactly what Christine Simpson told Bob – that Sue had probably suffered some kind of psychological trauma, but she's still our daughter and she knows who we are and that we love her as much as, if not more than, ever.'

Bob picked up as Sarah finished speaking. 'We're having some difficulty getting any idea of what may have happened. Christine advised us not to pursue the matter and put any pressure on her. That's the last thing we would want to do, yet we sense that she remembers more than she is prepared to tell us. On the positive side, she seems none the worse. Whatever it was that happened to her; she has a good appetite and had a sound night's sleep. However, she has hinted at a possible change of career plan. She is spending this year at a gallery in Cheltenham and is lined up for a fine arts degree at Durham. But now she is wondering about whether to stay on at the Galleria Europa and we wonder whether the past week's events have prompted that change of direction.'

Chapter Four

THE DREAM

Susanne drew a deep breath. 'What I am about to tell you is for your ears only and doesn't go beyond this room, okay? I doubt very much if either your parents or mine would take it – or me – seriously. They'd probably think I've had some kind of mental breakdown and be wanting me to see a psychiatrist. If you'd rather not hear me out, that's not a problem – I'll still be your friend and I won't be angry. It's just that I need to tell someone I can trust who is willing to believe me and I am not sure that my friends will be any different from Mum and Dad in their reaction. I know it's dumping a lot on you, and yet I think you can help me.'

She gave a big sigh, followed by a smile which

developed into an even bigger grin that broke the tension.

'We won't say a word,' Lydia declared, 'will we, guys?' 'Of course not,' Cecilia added, 'cross my heart and hope to die if I do!' Monty simply nodded and returned Susanne's grin.

Susanne's relief was very obvious. 'I don't know whether you ever wonder about the dreams you have. Usually, the minute I wake up in the morning, the dreams fade before I've even had my morning shower. It was quite different when I stumbled into that stone chamber last Sunday. I had the most powerful and compelling dream of my life and it is as real to me still as being here with you by a cosy log fire this afternoon.

'Anyway, it began with a far-off voice; a man's voice – calling out to me in the darkness. He called out 'Jennifer' three times, except the third time he called me 'Jennifer Cameliard' and said he needed to speak to me. I stirred from my sleep and asked him who he was and what did he want – I wasn't so much scared as curious. He spoke to me again, but this time he sounded much nearer. At the same time the darkness began to lift and a dim but growing light began to surround me.

'When he spoke to me again he was as close to me as I am to you and I sat up and saw a man wrapped in a cloak looking at me with a kindly expression on his face, and I knew that he would not harm me.

I recognised his face without being able to put a name to it, so I asked him once again who he was and what did he want?

He smiled at me in a most gentle manner, which warmed me through and through.' She stretched her hands towards the fire and then clasped her arms around her shoulders as if to reinforce the experience. 'He told me that he was King Arthur's friend, and my friend, too.' Cecilia was bursting to ask a question, but both Lydia and Monty shook their heads and she sank back in her chair.

'He said that he was Arthur's counsellor; that what he wanted was not important – it was what Arthur required that mattered and that he was simply Arthur's messenger. It was then that I realised I was talking to Merlin! It seemed impossible, but I had to ask him where Arthur was, and Merlin replied that he was not very far away but was still asleep at a place that was yet to be found.

'Then he said something even more amazing: that Arthur was calling him from across the ages, that it was a call to action which could not be ignored, since it was to fulfil the ancient promise that he would return when Britain had need of him with his companions and with me at his side. I found this hard to believe, since there had been other times when Britain was in danger – facing invasion, suffering from plague and civil war.

'Merlin insisted that this was the time and he reminded me that Camelot was destroyed from within by betrayal, mistrust, treachery and selfish ambition. He went on to say that men do not always make the best masters when they gain power over others, and that all too often the woman's voice is ignored. Then his voice suddenly became grim, and he warned me that the witch and enchantress would seek to create confusion and misery unless she is hunted down and restrained. I knew who he meant: Arthur's half-sister, Morgan le Fay – and I told him so. At this point he began to speak of what she would do once she knew that Arthur was abroad again; how she would be scheming to destroy him and use weak and foolish men to do her bidding. He said that my part at Arthur's side was to outwit her and frustrate her evil ambition. Then he asked me, a king's daughter, if I would play my part. There could be only one answer and I told him that if Arthur needed me, I would do whatever I could to help, provided that Merlin would be there to guide me.'

Susanne had been staring into the fire as she recounted all these words. Looking at the young faces before her, she continued, 'Merlin had a little more to say and asked me to remember the following:

> "In works of labour, or of skill,
> I would be busy too;

For Satan finds some mischief still
For idle hands to do."

'I wanted to know when Merlin would tell me that Arthur had been roused from his sleep. He promised to contact me but not 'in the land of dreams'. In the meantime, I was to bear in mind that it was vital to know my enemy and gain support from those I could trust, meanwhile I was to watch and wait. His last words to me were, "God be with you". Then he was gone. I think he may have returned again while I slept more than once, but he didn't speak or wake me up.'

Susanne sat back and rested her head against the pillows. She looked tired but gave her friends a smile of reassurance. 'I needed to share that with you and already feel much better knowing that someone else knows what happened after I went missing.' She glanced at her wristwatch. 'Mum will probably be wanting to bring the tea trolley in. I asked if we could eat here rather than sitting around the dining room table.'

'Can I ask a question?' It was Cecilia.

'Of course you can.'

'Why did the man in your dream call you Jennifer when your real name is Susanne?'

'Why don't you ask Lydia or Monty?' Her brother and sister looked rather alarmed.

'You tell her, Monty,' prompted Lydia. Monty looked at his sister and then at Susanne, who smiled by way of encouragement.

'It sounds crazy,' he hesitated for a moment. 'But I think he really said Guinevere, but it may have sounded like Jennifer in Susanne's dream. Guinevere was Arthur's wife – isn't that so, Susanne?'

'You're right, of course. Perhaps he is wise enough to realise that if I went around telling everyone that I was Guinevere I would have been taken away by men in white coats to the nearest mental hospital. The important thing is, do you believe that what I told you is true, or do you think I am mad?'

The girls were united in their reply, 'Of course you're not mad, Sue!'

'And how about you, Monty?'

'I don't think you're mad; it's just so weird – it means that Arthur and his men are going to be living in our world and that as Arthur's wife you'll be expected to join them. That's really awesome. What are you going to do?'

'Well, once I am really fit and strong – my usual self – I will have a good long think and someone will need to create a file using the internet to get as much background on Arthur, Merlin and Morgan le Fay for starters. So if you want to help, I would be happy to farm out some of that to you – I'll research Guinevere myself. Any offers?'

Lydia looked crestfallen. 'I'd really love to help you, Sue, but I am halfway through my GCSE course and have ten subjects to take next summer.'

'Of course, you mustn't let anything interrupt your studies. Monty, do you have any spare time, I wonder?'

'I don't mind having a go. Perhaps I could investigate Arthur and Merlin for you. Dad gave me his old laptop when I started at secondary school and although it's a bit slow, it still works fine.'

'Marvellous! So that leaves Cecilia, and I think that the best thing you can do, Cee, is to make use of the public library when you're next in town and ask if they have a simple introduction to Arthur and the Knights of the Round Table for someone of your age. What about that?'

Cecilia grinned from ear to ear. 'That's really cool. Mum often drops me off at the library when we go shopping in Charlton Kings and picks me up there when I have chosen my books. I know all about not talking to strangers and I usually see one or two of my school friends there in the children's section – so Mum doesn't mind.'

Just as Cecilia paused for breath, there was a tap and Sarah popped her head round the door. 'I hope you're all feeling hungry, because tea's made and if Sue can get the nest of tables out and move one or two chairs,

I'll put the food on the coffee table and then just grab a plate and help yourselves. If Monty and Cecilia don't mind sitting on cushions either side of the fire, there should be plenty of room for everyone.'

Chapter Five

THE HUNT BEGINS

Neither the Mortimers nor the Willoughbys would claim to be regular church-goers. When the issue was ever raised, they would describe themselves as 'once-a-monthers'. Following Susanne's return they had decided to attend Dowdeswell Church on Sunday morning by way of thanksgiving. They realised that there might be a journalist or agency photographer on the prowl, but as Sarah observed, 'We can close ranks around Susanne and politely say "No comment and no photo-call".'

As Gloucester's chief superintendent predicted, the posting of a police officer at the Mortimers' gate had been a sufficient deterrent and no further interest in the family was shown – with one exception. Miss M

Fairchild of Newsworthy Associates had made it her business to park well away from the Mortimers' house, and backing her own hunch, reckoned that there would be a service of Morning Prayer at about eleven o'clock. Arriving early, she slipped through the west door, accepted a prayer book and hymnal from the duty sidesman and sat over by the north aisle where she had a clear view of the door and the main body of the church.

Five minutes later the vicar (as she supposed), a woman in black cassock, white surplice, black scarf and academic hood, suddenly appeared from the front of the church and made her way to the west door to greet members of the congregation with a hearty 'Good morning!'. When the Mortimers arrived, flanked by another family, the vicar stepped forward and gave Susanne a hug, then stood back as they made their way to seats about half-way down the aisle. The two mothers led the way, with Susanne and three children following and the fathers bringing up the rear.

Morgan Fairchild had managed only a glimpse of Susanne's face. She turned to an elderly couple who had seated themselves next to her. 'She's looking remarkably well, isn't she, considering what she's been through?' The wife nodded in agreement. 'It's a mercy she was found before the cold snap arrived.

It would have been a funeral service otherwise, not Morning Prayer.'

The tolling bell died away, and the vicar welcomed the congregation and gave out various notices. No mention was made of Susanne's presence, which suggested that this was at the family's request. The only reference was in the prayers towards the end of the service, when thanksgiving was expressed for the happiness of the Mortimer family. During the singing of the final hymn, Morgan Fairchild crept out of her seat and left through the west door. Once outside, she hurried to shelter under a yew tree, where she took a camera out of her shoulder bag, determined to get some decent shots of Susanne, her parents and the family who were evidently providing additional support.

She waited for six or seven minutes, wondering just how many verses there could possibly be. Eventually, the church door opened and the parishioners made their way up the path to the lych-gate and either by car or on foot were homeward bound; but of the Mortimers or their friends there was no sign.

Morgan Fairchild returned to the church, which was empty except for the sidesman, who was checking the pews for discarded hymn and prayer books, and the lady vicar, who was locking the vestry door before coming down the main aisle. Seeing Morgan, she came over. 'I don't think we've seen you here before. It's a lovely little church, isn't it? Years ago, back in the 1950s, Princess Margaret would sometimes join the congregation for the early communion service, but that was before she was married.'

Morgan was nonplussed. 'Is there another door to the church? I thought there was someone I knew, but I must have been mistaken.'

'The only other door is the outside vestry door and sometimes when a person needs to leave in a hurry they let themselves out that way. It's a Yale lock, you see. Who was it you wanted to see?'

'I think I must have been mistaken. He was at the front of the church. I'm sorry to have wasted your time. Good morning.' She turned swiftly, made her way out of the church, muttering as she went, 'Curses on you, Susanne Mortimer, or whoever you are. You won't get away so easily. I've other strings to my bow. Perhaps a little chat with PC Bryan Holden might be profitable.'

Returning to her car, she cruised slowly past the neat hedge of the Mortimers' front lawn and saw the familiar figure of Bryan Holden sitting in the passenger seat of his patrol car. She parked behind him, walked over and tapped the passenger door window.

'How's my favourite police officer? It's Bryan, right?'

'PC Holden to you, Miss. What can I do for you?'

'I was going to ask if you'd like to have a friendly drink – perhaps even lunch – when you get off duty? It is the day of rest, after all.'

'Well, Miss … Fairchild. As it happens I am due to call in at twelve-thirty and my relief will then be on his way over. I'll need to nip home to change; the super would have me hung out to dry if I was caught fraternising with a young lady while in uniform.'

'That's not a problem – let's say one o'clock at the Hare and Hounds.'

'Right you are. I'll see you at the pub; the first drink is on me, alright?'

'If you say so, officer.' She gave him one of her sly smiles, walked back to her car and drove away.

✦   ✦   ✦

At Briar's Patch (a reference to the wilderness that confronted Douglas Willoughby when he was considering buying the derelict barn) the Mortimers had been invited to lunch.

'I don't want to embarrass Sue, but Clare, the children and I cannot let this opportunity pass without saying how delighted we are to have you here among us and asking everyone to raise their glasses and to wish you all that's beautiful, good and true in whatever the future holds for you – to Sue!' There was a clinking of glasses around the table, then Cecilia clapped her hands and nearly spilt her glass of grape juice.

'I expect you wish you were still back in Florence or Venice, rather than shivering in the Cotswolds,' Clare remarked.

'Not really. Italy can be just as cold as any English winter. I remember having to wrap up well when I went to St Peter's one Sunday afternoon last December. There was a queue to enter the basilica, and I wandered around, people-watching. Suddenly, there was a sound of police sirens coming in our direction. I asked a security guard what was happening. It was about four o'clock and the light was fading. He looked at me, guessed I was English or American, and replied, 'It is Papa; he is coming back to Vatican.'

'People were already being directed to keep the approach driveway clear, and a minute later four police motorcycle outriders came into St Peter's Square followed by a glistening black limousine. The interior of the passenger section was lined in white silk and illuminated with tiny white lights that made it seem like a fairy tale coach. The Pope was sitting alone in the rear seat, immaculate in his creamy-white robes and skull-cap, smiling at the crowds, giving his blessing as they broke into spontaneous applause.

I found myself caught up by their enthusiasm and began clapping – just as Cecilia did a moment ago – and crossed myself as he swept past.'

She stopped, gave a nervous giggle and said, 'Sorry, Douglas, I was rather carried away. It just made me feel so grateful that Mum and Dad and I have neighbours who are such wonderful friends. This is another moment to cherish, just as I cherish that brief encounter at St Peter's – and it was a jolly cold afternoon then.'

Morgan Fairchild was already settled in a window seat of the Hare and Hounds when Bryan Holden parked his silver-grey hatch-back, walked across to the pub and noticed her looking out, giving him a brief wave. He entered the lounge bar and made his way over to her table. 'What's your tipple, Miss …?' He seemed flustered.

'Please call me Morgan – and I can hardly call you PC Plod, can I?' He leant across the table and offered his hand, 'Bryan Holden at your service, Morgan. So what would you like?'

'Pleased to see you again, Bryan. A glass of sparkling water with a dash of elderflower cordial will be fine. I'm driving, you see. Can you pick up a couple of menu cards at the bar while you're about it, please?'

He gave her a boyish smile and moved across to the bar, placed the order and helped himself to menu cards and then studied the specials board. With the drinks paid for, he made his way back to the table, set Morgan's drink on the coaster and a menu card alongside it before sitting down.

'Cheers, Bryan! I hope you haven't broken some poor girl's heart on my account?'

'I don't have a girlfriend at present.'

'Oh goodie, so there's hope for me yet!'

Bryan sat back in his chair, looked at Morgan and without any change of tone said, 'I appreciate the chat-up line and I won't pretend I'm not flattered, but we both know that it's not me you're interested in, but any snippets of information I might be able to pass on. So tell me, why are you so anxious to learn more about Susanne Mortimer's activities this past week? While the church service was in progress I took a short walk and spotted your car, but you weren't in it. I asked myself why? I decided that unlike the other journalists, you probably had a personal reason for being there – am I right?'

'That's two questions, Bryan, and the answer is yes in both cases. She seems to have made a remarkable recovery in a very short space of time, having been without food or water for five days.'

'It may surprise you to know that the police are none the wiser as to what happened to her during that time and I very much doubt they will ever know unless Miss Mortimer chooses to say more – and that assumes that there is anything further to say. If I were you I'd take yourself back to London and tell your boss that you've drawn a blank this time and ask him for a new assignment. I don't mean to be rude, but I think I'll be off and pick up a hot pasty on the way home. I can recommend the steak and kidney pie laced with ale. The pub has a reputation for its catering.'

He picked up his drink, swallowed it, then stood up, nodded and smiled. 'Goodbye, Morgan, I've enjoyed our little chat but I doubt we'll meet again.' With that he left the building, climbed into his car and drove away.

Morgan sat by the window, tapping a sharp tattoo on the table with her fingernails. Her face was contorted with anger and frustration; it no longer conveyed feline attraction, but rather the features of a woman scorned and very dangerous to cross. She cursed under her breath, 'There's more than one way to skin a cat and if I have my way, Susanne Mortimer will wish she'd never been born. By Beelzebub, I swear it!'

To save the postman time, the Mortimers had a sturdy

mailbox bolted to one of the gateposts at the entrance to their property. Whoever was up and dressed first would collect any letters and place them on the hall table.

On Monday morning, Susanne wrapped up well and walked quickly down to collect the post. As she strolled back, she riffled through the letters, some of which were evidently cards for her. However, one carried no stamp and was type-written. She slipped it into her coat pocket and when she re-entered the house placed the other letters on the hall table. She hurried up to her room, opened the letter and felt herself shivering – not from the frosty morning air, but from a sense of apprehension. There was no address at the head of the notepaper, just MONDAY and the following message:

'SM, or whatever your real name is, I demand to know what happened last week: where you were and who you met and what you talked about. If you don't agree to meet me and tell me what I need to know, you'll wish you'd never been born, whoever you are. You have until the end of this week to give me the answers. I will ring at six o'clock every evening between now and Saturday to the public phone box where you live. If you do not pick up by Saturday evening, you will only have yourself to blame for the consequences – so be there. MF.'

Susanne sat down on her bed and felt herself shaking with fear, but very quickly the fear subsided and she felt a deep well of anger rise up inside her. She spoke with quiet determination, 'I don't know who you are, MF, but you've chosen the wrong person to try and intimidate – this girl doesn't scare easily!'

While Susanne was digesting the contents of the unpleasant message from MF, her father made two calls to Gloucester; the first to Christine Simpson and the second to Jackie Wilson. He renewed his invitation to them to join him and the family for tea at four o'clock. They had kept the late afternoon free and when Jackie raised this with the duty sergeant, she was advised that the chief superintendent was treating it as a duty visit and that she should charge the journey to the transport budget.

Christine and Jackie arrived within a few minutes of one another and were greeted by Robert, who had been asked to look after their coats and indicate where the downstairs cloakroom was situated. Sarah took the view that the lounge was a more people-friendly setting than the dining room. The family usually ate around the kitchen table, except when they had visitors.

Susanne was in her room, still uncertain which of two polo-necked jumpers to wear. Having made a choice, she slipped the chosen one on and then studied herself in the full-length mirror. The young woman who looked back at her was of medium height, slim build (but not skinny) her finely-chiselled features framed by a crop of luxuriant chestnut hair which fell to her shoulders. She was a beautiful young woman; a beauty inherited from her unknown mother and father. Satisfied that the cream polo-neck jumper suited her best, she tidied up her room in case of any unexpected visitors before joining the rest of the family and their guests.

Settled in the lounge, Christine and Jackie asked how Susanne was, having now been at home for three days.

'Remarkably well, all things considered,' Robert replied. 'She has a healthy appetite, sleeps without the need of any sedative and has been out walking with the children next door, with whom she is completely relaxed.'

'Has she made any further reference to last week?' Christine interposed. 'Not a whisper, beyond the shelter she stumbled upon on the Sunday afternoon. We haven't pressed her and she wanted to spend time with the children yesterday afternoon, which was welcome from our point of view as we needed to have a chat with their parents about one or two matters ...' He broke off, as he heard the vibration of footsteps on the stairs, and jumped up from his chair. 'That'll be

Susanne – I'll let Sarah know we're all here.'

The door opened and Susanne gave her father a quick hug and a kiss on the cheek before greeting Christine and Jackie, who had also risen to their feet.

'It's so lovely to see you again,' she exclaimed, and embraced Christine, kissing her on both cheeks, and then proceeded to welcome Jackie in like manner. Both women felt themselves blushing at her obvious display of affection, and Jackie responded by taking Sue's hands in her own, all the while shaking her head.

'I can't believe you're the same young woman I sat with last Friday. If you'll pardon my Anglo-Saxon, I'd say you look bloody marvellous!'

They looked at Jackie, then at each other, and burst out laughing. Christine, finding it hard to stop laughing, said, 'Jackie's absolutely right. You look really well, and I am so pleased for you and your Mum and Dad. Incidentally, where is your Mum?'

'Sue's Mum is right here, wondering what on earth this public disturbance is all about in the Mortimer household.'

Jackie blushed a second time. 'It's all my fault, Mrs Mortimer. I was carried away when I saw Sue looking so wonderfully well and happy.'

'You must be Jackie, and you must call me Sarah. Susanne's told me all about you,' then turning to Christine she said, 'and it's so good of you to come over to see us, Christine. Please, do sit down. I've made a pot of tea but if either of you prefer coffee, just shout. If Sue will hand out the plates, Bob can bring round the sandwiches, and do have as many as you like, so long as you leave room for the chocolate cake. It's home-made, and one of Sue's favourites.'

There followed a lively tea-party, punctuated by an account of all that had happened since Robert had brought Sue home.

Christine, gauging the mood of the occasion, put a direct question to Susanne, 'So what happens next? I don't need my stethoscope to confirm that you are sound in wind and limb. I gather from what your father told me on the phone this morning that you spent an exciting gap year soaking yourself in Greek and Roman culture, especially the Italian Renaissance Period.

Susanne responded after a short hesitation. 'Yes, I had a great time and I am so grateful to Mum and Dad for making it possible. Part of me wants to pursue it further; perhaps a fine arts degree. Part of me would like to continue working in the gallery. Then I begin to wonder if I am being selfish and that perhaps I should be doing some kind of charity work. I have some decent A levels and would like to put them to good use. I've been very privileged, living in a lovely home in a beautiful part of England with the best

Mum and Dad any daughter could wish for – it just seems to me I ought to give something back.' She looked a bit embarrassed, and then was quiet.

Christine gave Susanne a reassuring pat on the shoulder. 'I am sure you'll find the way forward and when it happens, you'll know it's the right thing to do. Whenever I'm undecided, I just offer it up.' Susanne looked puzzled. 'What do you mean?'

'I ask Him Upstairs to point me in the right direction – and it always seems to work out for the best.'

'And I'm sure that your visitors would love a piece of your favourite chocolate cake, Sue,' said her mother briskly, 'and if anyone wants their cup topping up, Bob will look after you.'

By five o'clock it was dark and Christine asked to be excused, so that she could feed her husband and teenage son. Jackie had a date lined up with her boyfriend. Susanne retrieved coats, scarves and gloves from the guest bedroom and popped the message from MF into Jackie's coat pocket. While she was upstairs, Robert took Christine aside and whispered, 'We'll be in touch to round off our concerns if that's alright with you?' Christine nodded and turned to thank Sarah for her hospitality.

'It's so good to see Susanne in her own home. She impresses me as a very sensible young woman. Thank you so much for inviting us over.'

Susanne came down and helped them with their coats, and as she did so, Jackie slipped an envelope into her hand – 'It's a note from one of the constables who made sure the media didn't bother you; he said it's self-explanatory.' Susanne slipped it into the back pocket of her jeans, gave Jackie a big hug and hovered by the door as her parents walked the two women to their cars. She gave a final wave and then hurried back into the house to escape the biting cold wind.

Robert and Sarah walked back, murmuring to one another, closed the door and returned to the lounge, where Susanne was gathering up the plates, cups and saucers while enjoying an extra slice of chocolate cake.

'Well, darling,' Sarah put her arm around Sue's shoulder, 'that went off very well. They are so natural and open – Christine's such a thoughtful person and Jackie, well she's just Jackie,' Sarah chuckled. 'But I am sure she'll be a good friend to you in fair weather or foul.'

'Thank you, Mum – and Dad, for making them so welcome. I'm so pleased they were able to see me when I wasn't …' She didn't finish the sentence, but recovered her composure and said, 'Why don't you both sit down while I get everything loaded into the dishwasher and find a home for the remains of the day? We'll probably feel peckish later this evening.' With that, she busied herself and when the lounge was cleared and her parents were watching the early evening news she announced that she was going upstairs to freshen up a bit, and then she would rejoin them. Closing her bedroom door, she pulled out the letter Jackie had given her and sat on her bed to study its contents:

Dear Miss Mortimer,

This is not an official letter but I thought it wise to alert you to someone who might cause a problem at some future date. I carried out much of the forty-eight hour police watch on your home yesterday and Saturday, to keep the Press away in accordance with your father's request for privacy.

Everyone co-operated with the exception of one young woman, who claimed to be a photo-journalist for a London news agency. She approached me and suggested that I might be willing to supply 'snippets of information' regarding your recent experience, with a hint of payment or other favours. I sent her packing. She turned up yesterday near the church, no doubt hoping for some pictures and persuaded me to join her for a drink at the Hare and Hounds when I came off duty. She pressed me again for any details of what happened during the four days you were missing.

Since neither I nor any of my colleagues are in possession of that information, I gave her short shrift and told her to take herself back to London. She was not very happy when I left. For your information she goes by the name of Morgan Fairchild, claiming to work for Newsworthy Associates somewhere in London. When I rang the number on the business card she'd given me on Saturday morning, I received the recorded message, 'Sorry, this number has not been recognised. Please try again.' I then consulted the BT yellow pages for that area and there is no entry for Newsworthy Associates.

Miss Fairchild is slim, dark-haired, has a certain feline attraction and I guess she's in her early to mid-thirties. She drives a black super-mini, registration number DC59 MLF, which doesn't show up on either the police database or the DVLA database in Swansea. I'm no expert, but I have a gut feeling that her interest in you is not charitable or sympathetic. I think you should watch your back if you ever meet up with her. I enclose my home telephone number should you need to contact me at any time about this lady.

With every good wish

Yours sincerely
BRYAN HOLDEN

P.S. Please thank your mother for the hot drinks and tasty sandwiches that she provided these past two days.
BH

Susanne scanned the letter a second time before replacing it in her pocket. She quickly flicked a damp flannel over her face and made her way back to the lounge, where she found her father still watching the news while her mother was skimming through the TV schedules to see if there was a programme they might like to watch together.

'I'm just hopping over next door to see the kids, okay? I won't be long.' She let herself out of the kitchen door and followed the well-worn short cut to the Willoughbys' house. On the way she decided not to mention the message from MF, but to share the contents of Bryan Holden's letter. When she reached Briar's Patch she made her way to the back door, tapped and let herself in to find Clare putting the finishing touches to the evening meal. 'Should I come back after supper, Clare?'

'Not at all. This has to go into the oven for thirty minutes. You might let the kids know that, please. Just go on through.'

When Sue entered the room, Monty and Cee abandoned the PlayStation and Lydia joined them as they gathered round her.

'I can't stay long – your supper will be on the table in half an hour – but there are one or two things I need to tell you.' Before she could continue, Monty said, 'Can I show you something first, Sue?'

'Of course you can.' Monty gave a slight cough. 'Well, I've already found out quite a bit about Morgan le Fay. Our history teacher has gone down with food poisoning and as there was no-one to cover a double period we were packed off to the library to catch up on any unfinished work. I had already completed my assignment, so I asked the librarian if I could do some research on one of the computers. I did a search and found a long article about Arthur, Merlin, Guinevere, Morgan le Fay and the Round Table. A lot of it was boring, but I saved the bits that I could understand and was allowed to run off one copy. As soon as I came home, I used Dad's copier to make another three.' He opened his school bag and handed round sheets of A4 paper to Susanne and his sisters. Sue took one look at the opening paragraph and then grabbed Monty and gave him a big hug, 'Oh, Monty, you are a clever Willoughby – no doubt about it!'

Monty blushed to the roots of his unruly mop of hair. 'It was no big deal.' That was clearly contradicted by the pleasure which his face displayed.

'I'm sorry, Monty. I didn't mean to embarrass you, but we can all take a look at your research straight away and get some idea of who we are up against. So heads down, everyone, and let's have a look at what Monty has produced.'

Chapter Six

A History Lesson: Unfinished Business

The Story of Arthur (in bits and pieces)
by M. Willoughby

The emergence of Arthur as a British national hero is deeply rooted in the country's history. Successive generations have been impressed by the dramatic stories told about him. One hundred years before he appeared on the scene, the Roman legions withdrew from Britain in an attempt to defend Rome as pagan tribes from northern Europe overran the empire's borders and began to advance towards its capital.

In the years that followed, other tribes – Angles, Jutes and Saxons – began invading Britain to carry off its wealth and then began to settle along the North Sea and English Channel coastal areas. Arthur was born in the last quarter of the fifth century AD. He was the son of the Romano-British leader, Uther Pendragon, who with the assistance of his counsellor, Merlin, had seduced Igraine, wife of the Duke of Cornwall. Igraine's husband was campaigning against the Saxons when he met his death and Uther was free to marry her and to raise their son, Arthur. Igraine had borne her first husband a daughter, known as Morgan le Fay, who felt a deep hatred for her step-father, Uther, and her half-brother, Arthur.

When Arthur was about 15 years old, he proved his right to succeed Uther as leader of the British by drawing the sword Excalibur from a great stone: a feat of strength which no other knight had been able to accomplish. Although he is usually known as King Arthur, this was probably the invention of writers in the Middle Ages. It is much more likely he was the 'Dux Bellorum' (the Battle Leader) of Britain and that he organised a mixed army of cavalry and foot-soldiers to halt the north European invaders. Arthur is said to have fought twelve decisive battles which checked the Saxon advance in southern England. Meanwhile, he created a Christian fellowship of knights known as the Round Table, who were pledged to defend their homeland and protect its people.

Throughout these years Morgan le Fay pursued her hatred of Arthur in various ways. She conspired with her sister's son, Mordred, to undermine Arthur's authority. She also encouraged Arthur's wife, Guinevere, to be unfaithful to Arthur by having an affair with his closest friend, Launcelot. By these means she weakened the ties that united the Knights of the Round Table. Morgan's hatred brought about a tragic outcome when Mordred rebelled against Arthur, and in the battle that followed both men were mortally wounded. It is said that Guinevere retired to a nunnery in the Wiltshire market town of Amesbury and was buried there. On hearing of her death, Launcelot, who died soon afterwards, arranged to be buried alongside her.

Over many centuries, myths and legends gathered around Arthur and the other major characters until the material was brought together by Sir Thomas Malory, who produced a comprehensive account of the life and death of Arthur in his *Morte d'Arthur*, completed in 1470 and printed by William Caxton in 1485.

England could have had kings named Arthur. At the end of the twelfth century, Richard the Lionheart nominated his dead brother's son, Arthur, to succeed him as king but Richard's youngest brother, John (of Magna Carta fame), had the boy murdered. Then at the end of the fifteenth century, Henry VII named his first son Arthur, but he died from natural causes and his younger brother, Henry, became Henry VIII. Both boys were 16 years old when they died.

The End

'That's wonderful, Monty, and has saved us a lot of time. Now it's my turn to read you a letter I received a little while ago from PC Bryan Holden. He was one of the police officers who stood outside our house over the weekend.'

For the next couple of minutes she read the letter and the children listened very intently to what the police officer had written. When she had finished reading, Sue said, 'I need to mention one or two things about the letter. Years ago, when I was at school, we were having an RE lesson about how the four gospels were chosen and why there were just Matthew, Mark, Luke and John. The teacher told us that there had been other accounts written, but they seemed to be less reliable and full of fanciful myths and legends – a bit like Arthur, really. But the teacher went on to say that there were some words of Jesus in these other accounts that may have been genuine sayings and she gave us one example – "He who is near me is near the fire".

I jotted it down in my exercise book and I've never forgotten it. Fire can do a great many things: it keeps us warm, it cooks our food, and it lights our way in the darkness – but there are two other things it can do – it can destroy and it can purify. My worry is that if you are seen too much in my company you may be in the line of fire in the destructive sense if this woman, whoever she is, wishes to hurt me. I would never be able to forgive myself if anything awful happened to any one of you because of her dislike of me.'

'Yes, but …'

'Sorry, Monty, no ifs or buts. There are things you can do, but we mustn't be seen together in public places if that woman is likely to be around. It would be too easy for her to set a trap for one or more of you to be caught and used to get at me. At present all she can possibly know is that we went to church together yesterday, but she didn't get any pictures of you because we left by the vestry door and were long gone before she realised it.

'When I get home I'm going to ring PC Holden to see if he can get a photofit of this woman, since he's the only one who has seen her at close hand. He may be able to do it officially if he can persuade his boss that the threat needs to be taken seriously. I'm saying all this not to frighten you, but to ask you not to do anything without checking with me first. Fair enough? Whatever you do, don't talk to any strangers.'

The youngsters agreed that Sue's advice was something they must accept. 'You will let us know if there's anything we can do, won't you?' Monty said.

'Of course I will; for starters would you like a trip over to Stonehenge on Saturday? Ask your Mum and Dad. We'd be leaving straight after breakfast and home before dark. Bye for now, I must dash.' Sue gave them a quick hug and left them to their thoughts.

When Sue returned home, she rang Bryan before joining her parents in the lounge.

'Hello, Bryan Holden here.'

'Hi there, Bryan, this is Sue Mortimer. I wanted to thank you for your letter and ask you a question, if that's all right?'

'No problem, Miss Mortimer, fire away.'

'First of all, please call me Sue. I assume from your letter that Miss Fairchild is breaking the law by using false number plates and committing a further offence by displaying a false road fund licence – is that right?'

'Absolutely right, and if we knew where the lady lives, we'd be taking action in respect of both offences – but we don't have an address.'

'Oh, I hadn't realised – how stupid of me. I had hoped that if she was arrested and had her car impounded, it would keep her out of circulation for a while and off my back.' She paused.

'My guess, Sue, is that she's in temporary accommodation somewhere in the Cheltenham area.' She heard a soft chuckle. 'Find the lady, Sue. We'll do the rest. I could then produce her message (which she'll deny all knowledge of) and bring everything into the open – except the pub encounter, perhaps. Sorry I can't be more helpful.'

'There's one more thing, Bryan. Now she's on your 'wanted list', as it were, would you be able to create a photofit picture of her? It would help me to know who I'm talking to if she suddenly confronted me unexpectedly. At present she has the advantage, knowing what I look like.'

'I'll see what I can do, but I can't promise anything. Contrary to popular belief, traffic offences are not at the top in the priority stakes as far as the photofit lab is concerned. You'd better let me have your mobile number rather than using your home number. It might worry your parents to get a call from me.'

Sue reeled off her mobile number. 'Thank you, Bryan. I do appreciate your support.'

'Any time. I'll be in touch. Goodnight.'

On Tuesday morning, soon after eight-fifteen, Clare

reversed her car out of the double garage and checked that the children had closed the front door securely before settling themselves in the car. Cecilia was the first to be dropped off on the school run. As the vehicle joined the early morning traffic west-bound to Cheltenham, Clare and her children were unaware that a black hatch-back was following them. At Charlton Kings, Clare made her way to the primary school, pulling into the kerb to enable her youngest to scramble out. The black car swept past them and Morgan pulled in some two hundred metres further along the road. She kept an eye on the rear view mirror, ready to move off as soon as Clare's car had gone past.

Clare drove towards Cheltenham to drop Lydia and Monty off at the state-aided grammar school, with the black car tailing them two cars back. The traffic in Charlton's larger neighbour was subject to a complex one-way system, which placed Clare on the outside lane ready to execute a right turn, whereas Morgan found herself boxed in on the inside lane and unable to follow the Willoughbys' car. A further obstacle was the traffic lights changing to red. Furious at losing them, she thumped her fist down on the steering column, which sounded a strident blaring of the car horn, attracting many hostile glances from neighbouring drivers. She shrank back into her driving seat while attempting to look apologetic, and found herself forced to turn left when the lights changed, towards Charlton Kings. She decided to stop off at the local library in order to consult the Electoral Roll to see if she could find out the identity of the family who had accompanied the Mortimers at Sunday's service.

Because she had not dared to park anywhere near the Mortimers' house, she had placed herself round a bend in the road and studied the occupants of each car that passed by. Most were driven by men on their own and it had been easy to spot the mother and children. The downside was that she didn't know in which house they lived. The Electoral Roll yielded the full names of those old enough to vote, and each of the houses flanking or facing the Mortimers' house. It was most likely to be the Naismiths or the Willougbys; but it might be the Lovelocks across the road. She also took the opportunity to consult the telephone directory to confirm that St Mary's C of E Primary School was within the state system. Morgan determined that she would target the youngster rather than her older siblings, who would be more suspicious if she made an approach to either of them.

Susanne had little difficulty in getting to sleep on

Monday night and felt completely refreshed when she rang Gloucester City Police and asked to speak to PC Jackie Wilson. 'May I know who's calling, please?'

'It's Susanne Mortimer; Jackie was detailed to look after me last week.'

'You're in luck. I'll put you through to the rest room.'

'Hi, Sue! I've just arrived back from sorting a domestic. A verbal disagreement that turned physical. How are things your end?'

'I'm fine. I just wondered if there's a chance we could meet for lunch some time this week – my treat?'

'How about today? I get an hour off at one and there's a comfortable eatery just two minutes away that does a great range of fast food, depending on how busy it gets. Their speciality (and my favourite) is 'baguette a la coronation chicken'. You can park here and I'll square it with whoever is on reception at lunchtime.'

'That's marvellous, Jackie. I'll see you at one.'

Sue had arranged the earliest appointment for her health check and shortly after nine-thirty she left her father's surgery, where his partner had given her the All Clear. Sue decided to visit the library to make a list of useful phone numbers and addresses. As she strolled along, well wrapped up and muffled against the cold wind, she noticed a black super-mini dart into a parking space that had just been vacated on the other side of the road. Idle curiosity became rapid attention as she noted the car's registration – DC59 MLF. She stepped back into an adjacent shop entrance so that she might not be seen but be well placed to study the driver's face. A young woman in a hurry slammed the door, locked it and began to dash across the road. Two cars refused to slow down for her benefit. She was, as Bryan had mentioned, an attractive woman, whose good looks were spoiled by the very clear irritation that her face registered as she walked into the library.

It was clear that Sue's intention could no longer be pursued. The library was a definite 'no go' area. Even as she acknowledged this, she realised that if she used her wits she might be able to shadow Morgan Fairchild back to her accommodation, provided the woman spent at least ten minutes in the library while Sue returned to her car and placed herself ready to follow Morgan. Eight minutes later, she was stationed half a dozen cars behind the black mini and waited. At ten o'clock her patience was rewarded when Miss Fairchild emerged from the library, hurried across to her car and joined the traffic bound for Cheltenham. Sue stayed in contact and hoped that she would not have to negotiate the town centre's one-way system. Happily, just before London Road became the High

Street, Miss Fairchild signalled right into Hewlett Road and some two minutes later parked her car outside a house, locked it and let herself in to an Edwardian property, which as Susanne coasted by was identified by a neat sign as 'Homelea' Bed and Breakfast.

'Bingo!' Sue exclaimed, as she carried on down the road and noted it was Albert Road. 'Thank you, Albert – you're the answer to a maiden's prayer. Not only do I know what you look like, Morgan Fairchild, I know where you're hiding out.'

There was little to be gained by hanging around, so she decided to head towards Gloucester and familiarise herself with those parts of the city where she might gain useful information. She parked off Southgate Street near the Waterways Museum and wandered, not aimlessly as she had done just five days ago, but with a searching eye and a clear purpose taking shape in her mind.

A few minutes before one o'clock, Sue returned to her car and drove to the Gloucester City Police Station on Bearland and parked in the visitors' designated area before making her way to reception. Jackie had made a quick change into casual clothes and linked arms with Sue as they headed for the fast-food diner. They found a corner table well away from the draughty entrance and Sue went over to the counter to order their food.

When she returned and they were both settled, she began talking. 'I think we've made a break-through where Morgan Fairchild is concerned. Bryan's letter,' she paused while she took it out of her bag and passed it to Jackie, 'makes it clear that she's driving with a false set of number plates and a false road fund licence disc. When I asked Bryan why the police had taken no action, he stated the obvious – they have no address for her and until we find the lady, there's nothing to be done. Anyway, you read the letter, then I'll tell you the rest after we've eaten our lunch.'

Jackie read through Bryan's letter – 'The crafty little so-and-so,' she muttered as she handed it back. They then began to enjoy their lunch. Susanne asked Jackie if she would like a cup of coffee and then went and collected lattés for them both. Susanne, with a twinkle in her eye, said, 'You'll never guess what I've done.' Jackie shook her head. 'Not the faintest idea.'

Chapter Seven

THE HUNTER HUNTED

'I've found the lady. I know what she looks like and I know where she lives!'

'How on earth …' Jackie exclaimed.

'Call it luck or justice – we nearly collided on our way to Charlton Kings Library, but I managed to duck out of sight before she could see me.'

'How do you know it was her?'

'She drove sharpish into a vacant parking space opposite the library, stepped out of her car and was stranded for about five seconds in the middle of the road because two cars refused to slow down for her to cross. I glanced at her car. It was black and its registration was DC59 MLF. The end result was that I tailed her all the way back to her accommodation in

Cheltenham – she's staying in a B & B called Homelea in Albert Road.'

Jackie's face was a picture. 'So we can pull her in?'

'It would help me if she could be taken in on Friday afternoon or early Saturday morning. I need to drive to Wiltshire on Saturday and it would be a relief to know she wasn't waiting to ambush me, since it's my scalp she's after.'

Jackie looked uncertain. 'Two things, Sue. Either we haven't had this conversation until Friday afternoon or it might make sense if we told Bryan, to see what he thinks. He knows what she's like and it seems only fair that you don't withhold this kind of information from him.' Sue recognised the sense in what Jackie was saying and realised that it was for Jackie and Bryan to decide how to handle the matter, not her. They decided not to have a second cup of coffee and, having checked their watches, realised it was time for Jackie to get back on duty. As they walked back together, Sue remarked, 'You know that the dark angel is ringing our local call box every evening at six, starting tonight with the final call on Saturday in order to set up a meeting between us? I'm not going to take the bait until Saturday. For a start, she could be hanging around waiting for me to arrive, with the intention of either snatching or attacking me. The other reason is to deliberately wind her up because when people become angry and frustrated they sometimes do stupid things. So I intend to take the call on Saturday and agree to meet her.'

'You what? You must be out of your cotton-picking mind!'

Sue laughed. 'I knew you would say that. The thing is, if I don't draw her out, I'll be looking over my shoulder all the time, and I refuse to become a victim. There's a saying that 'the best form of defence is to attack'. When she rings on Saturday she'll want me to meet her at a place and time of her choosing. I will tell her where and when I am prepared to meet her, and then put the phone down on her before she has the opportunity to respond.'

Jackie had a worried look on her face. 'That may seem a good idea, but I am not sure it's the answer and my hunch is that Bryan would think so, too.'

'I appreciate your concern, Jackie, I really do. When I spoke to Bryan last night it was clear that he is as anxious as I am to nail this woman before things get nasty. If you and he are willing, it might help things along if we had a meeting to sort out a plan of action. There's more to say, but we're out of time and you need to be ready for duty ten minutes from now.'

Sue settled the bill and they hurried back to the station, where they hugged one another before Jackie disappeared into the building. Sue made her way to the city public library's reference department and spent the rest of the afternoon consulting directories and making use of a vacant computer, accessing a substantial body of detailed information. She sat back and began to draft a 'catch-all' letter, limiting it to one sheet of A4 and then decided she'd done as much as she could. She walked back to the police station and drove home ahead of the early evening rush hour. She let herself into the house, to be greeted by her mother, who had heard the car coming along the drive. 'Have you been to the gallery to let them know you're fit for work – I gather you've been given the all clear?'

'No, Mum, I've been in Gloucester most of the day. I had lunch with Jackie and spent some time wandering around. Can we talk about this when Dad's here, please?'

'Of course we can – if that's what you want. Right now, how about a cup of tea and a last piece of chocolate cake?' On that, there was full agreement.

When Sue and her parents had finished their meal that evening, she gave a sigh, 'Mum and Dad, we need to talk. Can we forget the clearing away and just stay here, please?'

Robert glanced quickly at his wife and said, 'Of course we can, sweetheart.' Sarah felt herself tighten as she wondered what was to follow.

'I know the last few days have been topsy-turvy for all of us, but I think it's only fair to tell you how I feel about everything that's happened. When I woke up last Friday morning, I didn't have the faintest idea where I was or who I was – except that the initials JC were important and the notion that my name was Jennifer and not Susanne. I was still confused when Jackie and her sergeant caught up with me in the city centre.

'Christine Simpson couldn't have been more sensitive and understanding when she carried out her examination (it was such a relief to have a woman doctor). When she asked me questions, she did so in a very gentle way. As for Jackie, she was just what I needed – someone nearer to my own age who chatted about everything under the sun while I enjoyed my coffee and biscuits. I began to feel alive again. When Dad arrived and just held me, stroking my hair, the reality of who I was and who you are started flooding back. It was almost as if I had come back from the dead and when the cold front kicked in twenty-four hours later and the air temperature plummeted from thirteen degrees to below zero, I knew that I was lucky to be alive and that the line between complacency and catastrophe is very thin …' Her shoulders began to shake. '… it's alright, I'm not going to cry.'

Sue gave a sniff and her parents a brave smile before she continued. 'Anyway, ever since I've been home, I've come to the conclusion that whatever I do with my life in the long term, there's something I need to do right now. My life has been given back to me and when I see young people my age looking at the few vacancies on offer at the job centre, and how many more don't even bother looking because they are over-qualified or don't have even the most basic job skills, then I need the lesson I learned from my experience of last week to result in something positive.

'I need the local and national media on the back of my experience to help me set up a foundation training centre in Gloucester where I was found; I need the City Council to throw its weight behind this initiative; I need the business and commercial organisations to give me the benefit of their expertise; I want the community-based charities: Round Table, Rotary, Lions and Probus to come forward; I need recently-retired professionals whose careers have spanned everything from factory production, clerical work, catering, computer and IT skills, to volunteer their time and talent to staff and mentor all those areas of skilled and semi-skilled work. I need all the many charitable foundations that make grants to come forward and make money available so that the young unemployed may have the chance to make something of themselves on a one-year training programme, which like the NHS will be free at the point of delivery. Most of all, I want to identify a building large enough to accommodate classes of fifteen to twenty students in all the different skill areas; a building that doesn't require an impossible sum of money to make it fit for purpose at a peppercorn rent. I thought Douglas could help in that respect. There's only one thing wrong with my vision – it's not what I want that is the important consideration, but what the young people in this part of the country need that matters most.' Sue gave another big sigh, and then asked, 'Am I crazy to ask for so much? I just feel that last week's publicity, which was generated when I went on my walk-about, provides a once-in-a-lifetime opportunity to salvage something good out of what could have been a tragic event. Meanwhile, I love you very much.'

'Well, Sue, you certainly know how to take the wind out of our sails. Mum and I knew there was something going on, but never in our wildest dreams did we ever imagine anything like this.' Robert sat back in his chair and realised that the emotion coursing through him was exactly how he had felt when he had seen Susanne in the interview room in Gloucester – a mixture of anxiety and relief, of bewilderment and joy.

'Mum, I know you've been worried about me, but you don't need to worry any more. I promise. Now let's get this table cleared.'

Later that evening, she spent time talking with her father and asking if she could use the phone and his computer to e-mail her appeal as widely as possible. Robert agreed without hesitation and added with a wry smile, 'Even if nothing comes of it, sweetheart, at least you will be able to say, I did the best I could, and that is something of which you can be justly proud.'

For the next three days, Susanne was totally absorbed contacting a roll-call of individuals, companies, local government departments, employers and union organisations, charitable trusts, the press, TV and radio together, with personal visits to key figures by pre-arranged appointment. She also touched base with the local groups whose membership drew upon those of retirement age. The central plank of her appeal was that the young unemployed need help – practical help and encouragement – before they became lost souls in an uncaring world.

Where Gloucester leads the way today, other towns and cities may follow tomorrow. At the bottom of every letter and e-mail, a famous quotation was attached:

"Ask not what your country can do for you – Ask what you can do for your country." JFK, 1961.

On Wednesday evening she had a phone call from Cecilia, who sounded apprehensive but also excited. Earlier that evening, just as it was getting dark, her mother asked if she would mind posting some letters that had been overlooked when she left for the school pick-up run. Since it was just a two-minute walk, her mother felt her daughter would be safe, but insisted that she take Caesar with her. She set off along Glevum Close, with the dog pulling hard on the lead until he stopped suddenly to investigate an interesting scent. Cecilia noticed a black car parked under the street lamp at the corner facing towards her and on her side of the road. At first she thought it was unoccupied, but a movement in the nearside front seat gave a brief glimpse of a woman's face. She walked on past the car and round the corner to the pillar box some three hundred metres away. Having posted the letters, she set off for the return journey, much to the disgust of Caesar, who clearly had expected a proper walk.

When she turned back into the Close, she was surprised to see the woman standing beside her car and effectively obstructing the path. Cecilia considered crossing the road, but could see no good reason for doing so. Nevertheless, her pace slowed and as she glanced at the rear registration plate, she had a nasty shock. An overhanging tree cast its shadow over half the black-on-yellow lettering, but she could clearly make out 9 MLF – that was enough. Before she could decide what to do, the woman spoke to her.

'Hello, young lady. Do you live around here?'

'Why?' replied Cecilia.

'I'm looking for the Mortimers' house.'

'My parents said I shouldn't speak to strangers.'

The woman gave a strange laugh. 'I'm not going to hurt you.'

Caesar had started to growl.

'No, you're not, because if I let go of his lead, my dog will bite you if you lay a finger on me – and if you don't get out of my way, I'll ask my mother to dial 999 and the police will come and arrest you!'

It was quite evident that the girl's reaction was not what the woman expected. She shrugged her shoulders. 'See if I care, you stupid child.' She opened the car door, switched on the ignition, and after making a three-point turn, drove away – but not before Cecilia had satisfied her curiosity: it was DC59 MLF. Only when the car had disappeared around the corner and the sound of the car engine had died away did the girl realise that she was shaking.

Sue listened and then said, 'Have you told your mother?' Cecilia's voice had settled down and she said quite evenly, 'No, I thought I should speak to you first and the others agreed.'

'Thank you for letting me know – but I really think

you should tell your Mum and Dad. They will probably contact the police for their own peace of mind, and since you were sharp enough to take the car's number and get a good look at the woman, the police may want to talk to you. They already have a growing file on her activities in the area, which will do her no good at all. I'll have a word with PC Holden, who is the other person who knows what this woman is like.'

As soon as Cecilia had put the phone down, Sue rang Bryan to bring him to up-to-date with this new development and to ask what decision he had made about pulling Morgan in for questioning about her car. Bryan's reaction was swift: 'I think we must make use of the information we have regarding this woman, and I'm going to prepare a brief dossier which I hope will be acted upon by my superiors. If we bring her in for questioning, we can impound the car and get some fingerprint evidence from the steering wheel and see if we find a match with prints on the threatening message she delivered to you. We can try to establish how she obtained not only false plates and tax disc, but also where she bought the car. Her driving licence needs looking at, and we ought to check out her car insurance. Tonight's episode will certainly concentrate the minds of the people on the first floor and even if we can't take her out of circulation, we can make life very difficult for her in the next week or two.' He paused. 'It would be good if we could meet up with Jackie – how about Friday lunchtime at the café round the corner from the station at one?' Sue confirmed her availability and they rang off.

It was a working lunch and Bryan gave an account of the response to his report. Higher authority had instructed that two officers from the Gloucester station would visit the Albert Road guest house early on Saturday morning. Once they had established Miss Fairchild's ownership of the car, they were to bring her and the car back to Gloucester, where she would be questioned and cautioned. The car would be impounded for the purpose of examination. With reference to the threatening note, if a match was made with prints on the note and Miss Fairchild's on her steering wheel, a further charge of threatening behaviour might be prepared.

The duty officer on Wednesday evening had logged a call from a Mr and Mrs Willoughby (neighbours of the Mortimer family) saying that a woman answering Miss Fairchild's description and driving her car had acted in an intimidating manner towards their 11 year old daughter. She had obstructed her on her return home from posting letters that evening. The child's presence of mind had enabled her to get home safely. Bryan's conclusion was that this latter incident was likely to be treated more seriously than the note addressed to Susanne.

Before Bryan and Jackie returned to duty, it was agreed that Jackie would keep a low profile or, as she put it, be the ferret charged with trapping the rat in its bolt hole. In a parting shot, Sue invited her friends to check out the local evening news round-up on radio the following day.

A few minutes after eight o'clock on Saturday morning, a patrol car pulled up behind the black mini outside 'Home Lea'. Two police officers, a man and a woman, made their way to the front door of the guest house and rang the bell. The door was opened by a cheerful woman in her mid-forties. The sight of the two uniformed constables brought a look of alarm to her face – 'Has something happened to …?' PC Alice Harvey smiled reassuringly, shaking her head. 'We're sorry to disturb you so early in the morning, but can you tell us if the owner of the black mini is staying here?'

As relief flooded across the woman's face, she responded promptly, 'Oh yes, it belongs to Morgan, that's Miss Morgan Fairchild. Is something the matter?'

The other PC took over. 'We would like to speak to

her if that's not inconvenient.'

'I heard her moving about in her room. She asked for breakfast at seven-thirty as she has a busy day ahead of her. Perhaps you'd like to wait for her in the guests' lounge while I go and call her. Being November, she's the only visitor staying here, so you won't be disturbed.'

'Thank you, that would be most helpful.'

They were led into a comfortable room overlooking the road where the car in question was clearly visible. The proprietor invited them to sit down, then hurried up the stairs. She had left the lounge door open and the two officers could hear the voices, but not make out what the women were saying. Eventually, they came down and entered the room. 'I'll leave you to talk to Miss Fairchild, then.'

'Actually, Mrs …?'

'Oh, I'm sorry – it's Piper. Olive Piper.'

'Thank you, Mrs Piper. As I was saying, we would appreciate it if you could stay for just a minute or two. My name is PC Blake and my colleague is PC Harvey.'

He then turned his attention to Morgan Fairchild. 'Miss Fairchild, can I ask you to look out of the window and tell me who the owner of the black mini is?'

'It's mine. Why?'

He turned to Mrs Piper. 'I'm sorry to have taken up your time. Please feel free to leave us while Miss

Fairchild answers one or two more questions.' Mrs Piper smiled nervously and left the room.

'You asked me why I wanted to know if you are the car's owner. I have to tell you that the car is displaying a false set of number plates and a false tax disc. You should know further that it is a criminal offence to drive a car that is not properly registered and taxed.'

'You must be mistaken.'

'I assure you, neither the DVLA at Swansea nor the police central database has any record of the registration or the issue of the required road fund licence. May I see your driving licence, please?'

'Why? There's obviously been some mistake – computers are always spewing out inaccurate information. Good God! Only last week …'

'Miss Fairchild, if as you say there has been a mistake, then the sooner we clear it up, the better. Meanwhile, I need to examine your driving licence.'

She looked as if she was about to scream, but then her shoulders sagged. 'It's upstairs in my handbag. I'll go and fetch it.'

When she had left the room, PC Harvey went to the rear of the house and spoke quietly to Mrs Piper. 'We needed you to be present when we asked Miss Fairchild to identify her car. You are an independent witness and we may need you to make a witness statement to that effect. I'd better get back to the lounge.'

When she re-entered the room, Keith Blake was studying the piece of pink plastic, comparing the photograph with the face looking grimly at him. She was wearing a coat and scarf, clearly expecting to go out.

'I'm going to have to hang on to this for the time being, Miss Fairchild, and ask you to accompany us to the station.'

'What?' she yelled. 'That's absurd!'

'I think you fail to appreciate that you are committing a serious offence and if you are found guilty the prospect of a very heavy fine. If you are not willing to go to the station with us, I shall be obliged to formally charge, caution and arrest you. The choice is yours, Miss Fairchild.'

'But there are things I have to do,' she wailed. 'Can't I come along later?'

'Those things will have to wait, and I am sorry to tell you that until a thorough investigation has been carried out, your car will be impounded.' His colleague went over to Morgan. 'Will you come with us now? You can drive and I will give you directions to the police station. PC Blake will follow us.'

It was clear that further argument was futile. The officers thanked Mrs Piper for her co-operation and a minute later, the two vehicles were gone, en route to Gloucester city police station.

Chapter Eight

THE STONE CIRCLE

While Morgan was being questioned by the police, the Mortimer and Willoughby families were enjoying a leisurely breakfast. Douglas and Clare were happy to let the children join Sue for her trip to Stonehenge and soon after nine they walked over to the Mortimers' house, eager to be on their way. Sue's car was already out on the drive, and after farewells had been exchanged they drove away.

'Have any of you been to Stonehenge before?'

'Mum and Dad took us when Cecilia was a toddler.' Lydia turned to her brother, 'Do you remember much about it?'

'Not really. Most of what I've picked up has come from TV documentaries. They've been doing quite a lot about the excavations there during the summer holidays.'

'I can't remember a thing,' said Cecilia. 'We did a class project in year four about where the stones came from, how they were taken there and made to stand up. We had to make the stones in different sizes from polystyrene, which were then painted grey. Some of the smaller stones were bluish-grey. Then we put big stones on top and they were grey as well. The stones were formed into a big circle and stuck together with Bostick. The bluish stones made a smaller, inner circle. Then three sets of even bigger stones made a horse-shoe shape in the middle, and there was one last stone, which the teacher said was an altar, but she wasn't sure whether it should stand upright or lie flat on the ground. I think we decided to lay it flat in case it toppled over.

'When it was finished, it was taken into school assembly one morning and some of us had to read from a script all about the Stone Circle and why it was built. We even had a picture taken of us standing round the model which was printed in the local paper.'

'My goodness, Cecilia, what a wonderful memory you have! Now how about we switch on BBC Radio Two and listen to some pop music?' They joined in the songs they knew and the journey seemed to pass very quickly indeed. Just twenty minutes short of eleven o'clock, they arrived at the northern outskirts of Amesbury. Sue had already been in touch with the vicar, who assured her there were no records or other evidence to connect Guinevere and Launcelot with Amesbury Abbey, so they decided not to bother to visit the building.

At the major roundabout, Sue turned right onto the dual carriageway sign-posted to Exeter, and half a mile along they crossed over the other side of the carriageway and entered a narrow driveway to the cottage where her friend, Lucy Everdene, was based. As they were getting out of the car, Sue reminded them to take their anoraks with them, because it was bitterly cold and there was a strong wind blowing from the north. They began looking for the front entrance as Lucy came round the corner. She welcomed them in a very quiet voice, 'It's lovely to see you again, Sue, and to meet your friends. I'm Lucy, so do please come into the cottage and we can make introductions where it's warm – and thank you for bringing a dry day. Stonehenge, when it's wet and windy, isn't much fun at all.'

They followed her round to the back of the cottage and went in through the kitchen door and she ushered them into a large room, most of which was occupied by a very large table with chairs all around. On the table were cakes and biscuits, and Lucy asked them what they would like to drink. With the drinks served, she asked the children to introduce themselves. 'I'm Lydia. I'm the eldest, and I will be taking my GCSEs next summer. I go to the Grammar School in Cheltenham.'

'I'm Monty, and I'll be fourteen just after Christmas. I begin my GCSE course next September. I'm at the same school as Lydia.'

'My name is Cecilia, and I'm in my last year at St Mary's School in Charlton Kings. My Dad's an architect and he built the house where we live. What do you do?'

'I wear a number of different hats, but my main job is to encourage people who visit Stonehenge to learn as much about the surrounding area, as well as the Stone Circle itself, while they're here. I'm helped by volunteers who live locally and two or three young adults from Europe who stay with me here at the cottage for about six months.'

'From what I've read about Stonehenge,' Sue observed, 'most of the main developments were about four thousand five hundred years ago. Are there any sites around here associated with the Dark Ages after the Romans had cleared off back to Italy?'

'It's not an area I've studied in any great depth. There are Iron Age hill forts in southern England, of course, but the person you need to talk to is a professor from Oxford, who is actually studying the stones today. He's busy making a survey of sites where twelve major battles were fought between the British and the invading Saxons. But there are no connections with Arthur in this area. He's a bit off course, if you ask me!'

'If you and my gang don't mind, I'd like to go and talk to him if possible.'

'Why don't we all go over together?' asked Lucy. 'I assumed that you and the children might want to visit the Circle anyway, and being of school age English Heritage have given me a discounted price for them.'

'That's marvellous, Lucy, thank you very much.'

With that, they piled into Lucy's Land Rover and made their way to the Stonehenge car park. Lucy escorted Sue to the ticket turnstiles; they collected their receipt and walked through the underpass to emerge onto the grass perimeter of the ancient monument.

It was a bright, dry day but with a biting chill wind that stung their faces. The winter sun was low down in the sky and Lucy shielded her eyes as she looked across to the southern perimeter.

'There he is! That elderly gentleman by himself.' She pointed to a figure who was standing listening to the audio-guide. 'Why don't you go on ahead and we'll catch up after I've given these young people a potted history of the Circle?' Sue nodded her appreciation and set off round the circuit at a brisk pace. She caught up with the professor just as he was about to move on. 'Excuse me, but are you the professor from Oxford? You won't know me. My name's …'

'Jennifer, I believe, if I'm not mistaken.' Susanne almost staggered backwards at the professor's greeting. In a hesitant voice she asked, 'Merlin, is it you?' His reply dispelled any doubts. 'If it's not, then you've wasted your time and I've wasted mine.' It was said in such a kindly and gentle way that Sue realised no rebuke was intended.

'So,' he continued, 'what have you to tell me?'

She gave him a brief résumé of all that had happened since she had returned home, including a detailed account of Morgan le Fay's failed attempts to cause trouble. 'Right now, she should be in police custody, facing charges of misrepresentation, motoring offences, threatening violence and intimidating a minor.' She then gave a report on her initiative to create a skills training centre for Gloucester's young unemployed.

Merlin paid close attention until she had finished. 'You are to be congratulated on all counts, but tell me, who are the young people that I noticed with you when you arrived?'

'They are my dearest friends and the only ones

who know of our first meeting. I would trust them with my life.' She had barely finished speaking when Lucy and the children joined them. Sue called them forward. 'I'd like you to meet my friend Lucy, who works here, and these are my very special friends, Lydia, Monty and Cecilia.' As she spoke their names, the professor gave each one a courtly bow. There was a short silence, broken by Monty.

'Sue, there's something I've been meaning to tell you ever since we left home. I've found out something more about Arthur and Guinevere. Back in 1191, the monks of Glastonbury found the bodies of Arthur and his wife in the grounds of the Abbey near the Lady Chapel. They were in a double grave and inside the coffin lid was a great cross made of lead.' He paused while he pulled a piece of paper from his pocket. 'There was an inscription on the cross in Latin which read: "Here lies buried the famous King Arthur in the Isle of Avalon". '

The professor burst out laughing and clapped Monty on the shoulder. 'Balderdash and poppycock! Well done, Monty. Let me thank you for drawing that to our attention. Richard the Lionheart's brother had a son called Arthur, but died before his son was born. A few years earlier, the Abbey had been badly damaged by fire and the monks were in need of money. They hatched a cunning plan to raise funds.

They produced two bodies, manufactured a cross suitably inscribed, and Glastonbury became a place of pilgrimage, patronised by princes and paupers. Even the king and his consort paid a visit. One of the oldest tricks in the book, in my view.' The professor chuckled. 'The Abbey grew wealthy on its reputation until a certain Thomas Cromwell put in hand the overthrow of the monastic system, and confiscated its property. The Abbot of Glastonbury objected, and lost his head, while the Abbey itself is now no more than a ruin.'

Sue turned to the children and said, 'I'm sorry to abandon you again, but before we go to Amesbury for lunch, I need a few more minutes with the professor. I'll see you back at Lucy's cottage.' She took Lucy by the arm. 'I've found a couple of places in the High Street which serve hot meals. You're welcome to join us. I'm paying.' Lucy shrugged her shoulders. 'I'd love to, Sue, but I have a volunteer from Sweden joining us, and she's arriving at Salisbury bus station this afternoon, off the coach from Gatwick, and I need to meet her. Another time, perhaps. But thanks for the invitation.'

Susanne and Merlin excused themselves and walked off together. 'I have to be back in Oxford before it gets dark, so we must be brief. Until I find Arthur and we can speak face to face, I've no way I can tell what he plans to do. But whatever it is, it will need money, quite a lot of money. If I know him, he won't have gone into that great chamber or cave empty-handed; nor will his companions. They will be sitting, quite literally, on a king's ransom, and those treasures will have to be converted into today's money. Your friend Lucy might well be able to find out from her employers which London auction houses might be approached to handle a substantial and valuable collection of late Romano-British treasures, but in such a way that doesn't compromise our identity. For the time being, use all your wit and wisdom in dealing with Morgan. If she can be confined or restrained in these next few months by the weight of the law, for any and every offence she commits, our task, yours and mine, will be that much easier to discharge. When Arthur hears of all that you have done, I am sure he will welcome you with open arms.'

Susanne felt her face colour up at Merlin's closing sentence. 'I understand what you say, but Arthur will be expecting to welcome his wife, Guinevere. I am Susanne Mortimer, I am 19 years old. I am not Guinevere, nor am I sure I could step into that role.'

Merlin looked at her with compassion in his eyes. 'You are being called to occupy that vacant seat at Arthur's table, a seat that demands more from anyone than can be imagined. It is called the Siege Perilous.

I may not be able to think a woman's thoughts, and will not attempt to do so. What I do say is this: you have displayed the courage, determination and spirit of Guinevere in the short time since we last met. So I, Merlin, say to you: do not be afraid. I am always with you; our hearts will keep in touch with one another. When you next see Arthur, you will know what is the right thing to do, and so will Arthur. Today was no accident. Remember that, and go in peace.'

They walked back together and the children were waiting to leave as Susanne gave Lucy a warm hug. Merlin clasped Susanne's hands firmly and then turned to the children, bending to speak to each one in turn and whisper something to them. With that, Sue and the children made their way down to Amesbury.

✦   ✦   ✦

The journey back to Gloucestershire was uneventful. The combined effects of the chill fresh air followed by a hot lunch left the children feeling a touch sleepy, but not before they had quizzed Sue about her connection with the professor. Not surprisingly, it was Cecilia who asked, 'Sue, have you met the professor before? You seemed to act as if you had.' Susanne didn't reply straight away. It was as if she was wondering what to say. 'If I answer your question, will you all answer one I'd like to ask you?' To her surprise they all agreed without hesitation.

'The professor is the man who visited me at Arthur's Stone – he is Arthur's counsellor, Merlin. There – now it's your turn. What did Merlin say to you, Cecilia?'

Cecilia replied, 'Just five words: Look after her for me.'

'And you, Monty?'

'Exactly the same.'

'Lydia?'

'Look after her for me.'

Sue was concentrating on the road ahead, but there was a fleeting look of comfort and reassurance on her face as the thrice repeated instruction was delivered. 'I am sure you will, and you know I will do exactly the same – I'll look after you all. Today has been more important than perhaps any of us can realise. I think Merlin is already looking to what lies ahead, and planning what preparations need to be made. I am sure it has something to do with the closing words of that book which Monty researched on the internet. Merlin has been trying to locate the sites of the twelve battles where Arthur defeated the Saxons.'

'What words are you talking about,' Monty asked.

'I found a copy of *Morte d'Arthur* in Gloucester City's reference library, and near the end of the book

Sir Thomas Malory writes:

"Some men yet say in many parts of England that King Arthur is not dead, but by the will of our Lord Jesus in another place until Britain has need of him."

'I think Merlin believes he'll find Arthur at one of those sites, and it's my belief that the time Malory speaks of has arrived, and that Merlin is preparing for his return.'

✦   ✦   ✦

Shortly after four o'clock, they arrived back at Glevum Close. Sue had a quick word with Clare to thank her for the loan of the children. Clare gave Lydia a knowing look, to which her daughter responded, 'Thank you very much, Sue, for taking us to visit Stonehenge. We really enjoyed it, didn't we, guys?'

'The pleasure was all mine. I really was glad to have your company – but I must be on my way. See you soon.'

As Sue walked back to her car, she heard Clare saying, 'You must tell us all about it over tea.' When Sue let herself in to her own home, she could hear her mother in the kitchen and the clink of cups. 'I'm back, and I hope you are not washing up, because I could murder a nice cup of tea.'

'Darling, have you had a nice day out with the

youngsters? How is your friend Lucy?'

'Yes to the first and Lucy's fine to the second. It's been an interesting day and the kids enjoyed themselves.'

'Come through to the lounge.' Sarah emerged with the tea tray. 'It's been quite cold here; it must have been very fresh up on the Plain. I'll let Dad know you're back. He's been clearing up the last of the beech leaves. He's convinced they do more harm than good because they never seem to rot down.'

Sarah left the room and Sue curled up in her favourite armchair near the open fire and felt tiredness creeping over her, while at the same time she knew she had to face down Morgan Fairchild later that evening. She heard her father's voice and then both her parents joined her and they enjoyed a companionable tea together.

'How did the youngsters rate Stonehenge?' Robert had wrapped his hands round his mug and as if to justify the action said, 'It's been cold enough here to freeze the proverbial brass monkey.'

'I don't know what they expected, but Lucy is top of the popularity stakes. She laid on cakes, biscuits and soft drinks to suit their taste. I must write and say a big 'thank you' to her for being so hospitable. She also gave them a personal introduction to the Stone Circle, having arranged a special price for us to go round it: just ten pounds for the four of us, bless her. We met an Oxford history professor while we were there, and they hit it off with him remarkably well. I daresay they're telling Douglas and Clare all about their day right now.'

Her father cut in, 'Speaking of Douglas, he took a look at some of those warehouses down at the Gloucester Docks. In addition, you've a stack of letters and e-mails to look at. I've printed off the e-mails and they're clipped together alongside the letters. After making the headlines last week in the local press, it looks as if you're going to be on page one again next week!'

Susanne's face flushed with excitement. 'That's great. Sometimes I think I must be crazy – but until I've had a chance to read the mail, I'm not going to count any chickens. Just one thing – are we eating at the usual time this evening? I need to go out for a few minutes just before six o'clock, but I won't be long. Oh, and another thing, are you going to be free for an hour or so early tomorrow evening? It would mean eating later, I'm afraid.'

Sue's mother looked at her, 'I must say you're full of surprises lately. Racing from here to Gloucester and back almost every day, then off to Stonehenge. Now what?'

'BBC Radio Gloucestershire want to do a half-hour slot after the evening news summary tomorrow about the foundation training centre in their *Facing the Future* series. They've flogged climate change and global warming for all they're worth, and they've asked me to do a one-off on the training project. What gave me the idea? How will it be financed? What sort of numbers do I expect to sign up, etc? It would be so good to have you there to give me some moral support. I need to be there by five forty-five.'

Sarah gave Sue an indulgent smile. 'You know we'll be only too happy to come along. In fact, Bob, why don't we make an evening of it and dine out in the city afterwards? All those present say 'aye'! We'll book a table for seven-thirty.'

'Thanks a lot, Mum. Do you mind if I have a bath now? I'm still a bit chilled and I could do with a real good soak.' She stood up, stretched and then made her way upstairs. She rang Bryan Holden. 'It's Sue. What's the latest on the wicked lady?'

'She was brought in for questioning and claimed that she'd bought the vehicle from a used car dealer in Cornwall, but can't remember his name and there's no record of the deal in the car. She said the paperwork is back home in Cornwall. We did get a set of matching prints with the note she sent you. When we challenged her, she dismissed it as a harmless joke – some joke! We've also confiscated her driving licence while it's being checked out so that will clip her wings. She's been advised of her rights and has dispensed with a legal representative. At present, it's likely she'll be charged with motoring offences and threatening behaviour towards a minor, which she denies and says the child was hysterical. However, given the prevailing public concern about child protection, she may be held overnight. She was still there when I came off duty after lunch.'

'Thanks a lot, Bryan. I've been wondering about her most of the day; whether she'll make the call this evening.'

'Why don't you forget about it, Sue?'

'I need to draw her out. If she gets the message that I don't scare easily, she'll either back off or do something reckless.'

'That's exactly what worries me. Just watch your back and let me know how the call goes.'

Chapter Nine

CRUNCH TIME

When she had put down the phone, Susanne sat on her bed and looked through the letters and e-mails. It was a mixed response from enthusiastic support for her proposals to a luke-warm encouragement but with an unwillingness to be involved in the project personally. Nevertheless, those prepared to give active support accounted for more than eighty per cent of the replies she had received, and for Sue that was sufficient encouragement to move forward. An hour later, fresh from a relaxing bath and well wrapped up against the cold night air, she made her way to the call box. In one hand she carried a powerful torch, and her mace spray in the other. There was no-one around and still a minute or two to go when she reached the kiosk. She walked on past for a hundred metres or so, and then turned back and waited in the shadow of a tree a few metres from the call box until the phone rang.

Spot on six o'clock it rang. Clearly Morgan was no longer helping the police with their enquiries. Susanne opened the door and picked up the phone.

'Is that Susanne Mortimer?'

'Speaking.'

'We need to meet.'

'I've nothing to say to you.'

'Just shut up and listen.'

'I'm listening.'

'There's a pub on the corner of Albert Road in Cheltenham at the junction with Wellington Road. Be there at seven o'clock tomorrow evening. Is that clear?'

'It's clear, but I've changed my mind.'

'What?'

'You heard. If you want to see me, be at the BBC studios in London Road at six o'clock tomorrow evening. Don't be late! Is that clear?' She replaced the phone on its rest and used her shoulder to open the door, clutching her torch and spray just in case. She marched home in a determined manner, 'Two can play at your game, Miss Fairchild,' she muttered to herself. She opened the front door and called out,

'I'm home. Shall I lay the table?' She then made a brief call to Bryan in her bedroom.

As the area weather forecast marked the close of Radio Gloucestershire's Sunday evening news round-up, a small invited audience was seated in the Blue Meeting Room. Facing them on a small dais was a table with a carafe of iced water and two glass tumblers, behind which two chairs had been placed. At six-fifteen a red light came on behind the dais and a young man came forward and took his seat behind the table.

'Good evening and welcome to this week's edition of *Facing the Future*. My name is Andy Powell and for those of you listening to this programme for the first time, we aim to examine through the eyes of professional observers and hands-on practitioners the issues that affect what the future may hold for us and our families in the region.

'Tonight; an invited studio audience, and you at home will have the opportunity to listen to a remarkable young woman who has a story to tell and a vision to share with everyone living and working or (perhaps more importantly) not working in the Radio Gloucestershire region. Two weeks ago she was on the front pages of our local and national newspapers.

If she has her way, she will be making headlines again in the coming days and weeks as she seeks to make her vision a reality.

'Two weeks ago a young woman disappeared in the Herefordshire hills while out walking with her family. Her disappearance sparked off a major search operation which failed to find any trace of her. Five days later she was seen wandering in one of Gloucester city's shopping malls. Please welcome Miss Susanne Mortimer.' Andy Powell stood up, and as Susanne stepped up to the dais he showed her to her seat. Susanne was wearing a pale cream linen suit and a sea-green chiffon scarf fastened on her left shoulder with a silver and turquoise clasp. She wore just a slight hint of make-up. Her burnished chestnut hair tumbling onto her shoulders framed her classic good looks. She attracted attention as well as applause. The two chairs had been arranged in such a way that she could look at the presenter as well as seeing and being seen by the audience.

'Thank you very much. If it's not a problem, I'd prefer to stand. I think better on my feet.' She looked out at the people sitting in front of her, smiling as she did so with no sign of hesitation or nervousness. 'It's very good of you to give up your evening to listen to my story and I hope that you won't feel it's been a waste of time. Until today I have declined to give interviews about my five-day disappearance. Initially, I needed to recover and spend time with my parents. Then, as the weather changed from the unseasonably mild spell of two weeks ago to the bitter, freezing conditions that we have experienced since then, I realised how close I had been to dying. The irony of my narrow escape was that on that Sunday evening I took shelter in a derelict box tomb which protected me from the wind and rain. I was completely exhausted and fell into a deep sleep, waking up early on the Friday morning. I suppose you could say I rose from the dead. Ever since then I have had a growing sense that the fact I survived had to be for a reason. The newspapers reported that I come from a privileged section of the local community, by which they mean I belong to the 'haves' rather than the 'have-nots'. The real privilege is to be the daughter of a mother and father who are the kindest, most loving and caring parents any girl could wish for – the material comfort is secondary to the love of my parents.

'It became increasingly clear that my life was not just about me but concerned the many hundreds of young people of my age who find themselves without a job or the hope of a job; without the opportunity of gaining basic skills or a reason for getting out of bed in the morning. Unless there is concerted action at every level, and across the widest spectrum of our local community, these young people will become lost souls, losing the will to want to work and dependent upon the benefit system for an indefinite and uncertain future. I believe this is wrong and feel sure that many others here in Gloucester and the surrounding area share that belief.

'During this past week I have been in touch with like-minded people by phone, letter, e-mail and one-to-one meetings with a specific and practical proposal. This is the creation of a training centre in the heart of Gloucester city offering a one-year foundation skills programme, free at the point of delivery and attracting the statutory training allowances provided by central government. It will be staffed by retired but experienced professionals from industry and commerce working on a voluntary basis.

'As of this evening, there has been an eighty-five per cent positive response from those I have canvassed and the lease of a property in the docks area of the city on a five-year term (open to renewal) at a peppercorn rent of fifty-two pounds per annum. In line with this level of encouragement, I have suggested that when it opens in the New Year it be known as the "Camelot Foundation Training Centre". Who knows? It might attract a grant from the other Camelot.'

Bob and Sarah were astonished at the assured manner in which Susanne addressed the audience.

She spoke without notes and with a maturity and confidence beyond her years. Where had it come from? As they mused upon this, Susanne invited questions. A woman who had crept in just as Andy Powell was making the introductions and taken a seat at the back of the room, stood up in the pause that followed Susanne's invitation. Andy Powell asked her to identify herself and put her question.

'I'm Morgan Fairchild, representing the London-based Press agency, Newsworthy Associates. Would Miss Mortimer care to tell us what actually happened during those five mysterious days? For all we know she might have been snugly settled in some Herefordshire farmhouse drawing up this Utopian fantasy.'

While Morgan continued to undermine Susanne's credibility, Andy Powell made a quick check of the invitation list and looked up as a studio technician passed him a slip of paper. He interrupted Morgan, who was being greeted with cries of 'Shame!' and 'Sit down, won't you?'

'Miss Fairchild, we are reliably informed by the Gloucestershire police that you are not a journalist and that there is no such news agency as Newsworthy Associates. It is you who are fantasising. You are not on the list of invited guests. This is private property and you will be escorted from this building by members of our security staff. The next question for Susanne

Mortimer, please.'

Two uniformed security guards entered from the back of the room and moved towards Morgan. 'Don't you dare touch me! I'll sue the BBC for assault.' They continued towards her, their arms linked together to form a human barrier and to drive her towards the door without using direct restraint. 'We are not going to touch you, Miss Fairchild, unless you attack us, but you are leaving the BBC's premises, and that's final.' She had no option but to retreat and finally turn on her heel and leave the room. The guards closed the door behind them as they followed her out.

There was an excited buzz, and then Susanne said, 'I'm sorry for that interruption, but for reasons best known to herself, Miss Fairchild has taken a dislike to me. However, that's her problem, not mine. I'd be happy to respond to any questions you may have.'

For the remainder of the programme Sue took questions from the floor, and by the relaxed way in which she dealt with them, demonstrated how clear-sighted and focussed her research had been. Andy Powell glanced at the clock and realised it was time to wrap it up. 'Ladies and gentlemen, Susanne expressed the hope that you would not feel this evening had been a waste of time. Judging by the probing questions you have asked, and the manner in which she handled them, my guess is that she has fully justified her conviction that her vision is well-founded. I have just one final question to put to her: Susanne, this undertaking is far beyond the capacity of one person to direct. How do you see it operating in practice?'

'We have created a board of trustees: twelve people of proven ability from across the various bodies that have an interest in supporting and guiding the project, and I am delighted to tell you that Councillor Chris Witham, the Mayor of Gloucester, has agreed to be chairman of that board. What we and all those who have responded have done is to put words into action. Thank you for the opportunity to share the vision with you.'

The audience was reluctant to leave, so Susanne joined them and was soon surrounded by those anxious to speak to her. Eventually, Andy Powell detached her from the group she was talking to, and with an apologetic smile, Susanne excused herself and followed him to the main control room where her parents were being given a brief introduction to the business of radio broadcasts.

'I've rescued your daughter from her instant fan club, and I want to say what a professional impact she made – not only upon the audience, but the BBC technicians and support staff. In response to our colleagues in Bristol, we had two wide-angle webcams, one at the rear of the meeting room, and one behind the dais, so we have you on both sound and vision. I have arranged for a CD format of the programme and a DVD to be sent to you, which may be helpful in the promotion of the Camelot Foundation's work. I've cleared this with the managing editors here and in Bristol. An acknowledgement of the BBC's support would be appreciated at any public showing.'

Sue felt someone tap her on the shoulder. She turned to see Jackie Wilson give her a sly wink as she said quietly, 'Bryan passed on the message you gave Miss M, so I thought it might be useful for me to be waiting in the wings in case of trouble. I slipped the technician a note of her bogus profession, which Andy used to good effect. Must love you and leave you.'

She moved away and shortly afterwards Sue and her parents took their leave of Andy Powell and headed for the restaurant, where a table had been reserved for them.

The Monday morning papers carried a full account of Susanne's presentation. Many had spiked the earlier page one headline and in its place were two pictures: one of Sue preparing to take questions, the other an unflattering picture of Morgan in full spate.

The overwhelming consensus of commentators was to congratulate Susanne's bold, commanding and practical determination to get things done and make things happen. As one columnist expressed it: 'Behind every great enterprise in the history of humankind, you are likely to find one person who asked the question, 'What if?' and then provided the answer 'Why not?' However young or old, wise or simple, rich or poor we may be, Susanne Mortimer has reminded us that there's always room for any one of us to ask the same two questions.'

Meanwhile, Sue was already on her way to the Europa Gallery, where she had negotiated a part-time workload of mornings only so that she could be in Gloucester every afternoon overseeing the countless demands of bringing Camelot into being. Throughout the day, Susanne was having to deal with the exposure which the previous evening's programme had created, and wondered which one of her friends or member of the Europa staff had given the press her mobile number. Switching it off wasn't an option, since it could jam a call from someone with an active interest or existing involvement in the Camelot Foundation. Even so, she reminded herself of the value of Press support.

When Susanne arrived home on Monday she found a hand-delivered letter for her on the hall table,

addressed 'to Sue' from Monty. She went into the
lounge, opened the letter and studied its contents:

Dear Sue,

We watched you on TV last night and everyone
thought you were really great. We felt so sorry
for you when Miss Fairchild started criticising
you, but were glad it didn't put you off.

I expect you've seen today's papers with
pictures of you and Miss F. The more I look at
her face, the more I think she must be a very
unhappy person. According to one newspaper,
she's already in a lot of trouble with the police.
I know she's trying to make trouble for you and
that Merlin doesn't trust her, but perhaps she
needs help?

Have you thought about asking her why she
seems to dislike you so much when all you are
trying to do is help young people? Perhaps if I
were to be with you it might be worth asking if
she'd like to talk things over – but somewhere
safe, like McDonald's or KFC. I haven't said
anything to Lydia or Cee about this.

Monty

Prompted by Monty's note, Susanne picked up the papers in the magazine rack. He was right, of course. There was Morgan, looking desperate and wild-eyed in contrast to her own assurance and composure. But as for getting Monty involved, that was a no-no – or was it? She went over to the phone and rang the Willoughby's number. Clare picked up.

'Hello, Clare, it's Sue. Am I interrupting?'

'Well done last night, Sue. We were most impressed. No, you're not – to answer your question. The kids have just finished loading the dishwasher and clearing away. Can I help?'

'I wonder if Monty could nip over for a few minutes? If he's busy, tell him not to worry. I'll catch up with him sooner or later.'

Sue heard Clare calling out, 'Monty, can you pop over and see Sue? She'd like a word.'

There was a click as Clare picked up the phone. 'He's on his way. Bye-ee.'

Sue met him halfway. 'Let's go into the lounge. The parents are out in the kitchen putting the finishing touches to one of Dad's favourites – sticky toffee pudding.'

They sat down either side of the fire. 'Thank you for your note about Morgan. The truth is I've been more than a little worried about what she might do to make trouble for me from the day I returned home. I still don't know what kind of harm she intends, but at present she's the one with bigger problems. Yes, she does look a very driven and unhappy woman, and I don't think it's an act.

'We have to assume it springs from the circumstances surrounding Uther Pendragon's seduction of her mother, Merlin's involvement in that event and the birth of Arthur. It sounds crazy, talking about someone who lived fifteen hundred years ago. The bottom line is that Merlin wants to find Arthur and so does Morgan. Merlin warned me she would cause trouble and that's clearly true. You think we might do better if we try to understand why she is so unhappy and the more I think about it, the more I feel you may be right. Merlin's track record in his dealings with women has been unsatisfactory, which is surprising when I consider how kind, gentle and understanding he has been towards me.

'However, it is possible that a friendly and more positive approach to Morgan might be the answer, but – you know what I'm going to say – not at the risk of putting you or any of the Willoughby clan in danger. So what do you have in mind?'

Monty looked into the fire and then at Sue. 'Would it be possible to write to her and just sign myself Monty with no address to identify and no mention of my knowing you? I could pretend to be a young unemployed person, which is true in a sense. I am young and I am unemployed. I could ask her straight out why she's unhappy and why she thinks so badly of you.' Monty sat back in his chair.

'Delivering the letter is no problem because we know where she lives. If she wants to reply, it has to be by a fool-proof method. If she thinks you are likely to sign up for a training course, then the Centre is the obvious answer. I can make sure that any letters addressed to you come straight to me: then we can take it from there. But let's sleep on it, and if we think it's worth trying, we'll check it out with your Mum and Dad.'

Monty sat up straight. His face had turned suddenly pale with alarm. 'They're bound to say No.'

'Not necessarily, Monty. The only people who would be in on this are you, me and your parents. Say nothing to Lydia or Cecilia. What they don't know can't hurt them. I'll be seeing your Dad at the Centre tomorrow afternoon and I'll raise it with him then. Meanwhile, Mum's the word!' Sue gave him a broad grin and put her index finger to her lips.

Monty stood up to leave. 'Fair enough, Sue. Thank you for taking it seriously. I wish more adults were like you. Anyway, I'd better be getting back, as I have an assignment to finish before tomorrow morning.'

Chapter Ten

COMING TOGETHER

The Camelot Centre, as the new foundation became known, took possession of the four-storey Council-owned warehouse the day after Susanne's broadcast. It was a wise choice. A year earlier, a developer had entered into a rental agreement with the Council to convert the warehouse into twenty-four self-contained units suitable for sub-letting to commercial and light industrial enterprises. Electricity, gas and water had been reconnected and ducted central heating installed. The units were complete except for being decorated according to prospective clients' requirements.

The developer's timing could not have been worse, however, as the country entered the global recession.

He had borrowed beyond his means and could not service either the bank loans or the Council rent because the expected start-up ventures were not forthcoming. The Council repossessed the warehouse and the developer went bankrupt.

In the weeks leading up to Christmas, a committee drawn from the Trustees and staff met each Monday afternoon to decide the allocation of units and organise the decoration. The building and construction department, including an area for auto repair and maintenance workshops, was on the ground floor. On the first floor a catering department and dining area occupied two-thirds, while the remaining third was set aside for a hair-dressing salon and a compact print workshop and art studio. The floor above was given over to an IT and secretarial skills department. The spare capacity was set aside as a small gym for staff and students. The top floor housed all the administrative sections of the Foundation – finance, registration, time-tabling, publicity, appeals – each with its own dedicated space. A main conference hall and two small committee rooms were created for day to day meetings.

The response from charitable trusts and grant-making bodies had been far beyond Sue's expectation. A retired solicitor had produced a draft constitution in order to secure charitable status for the training centre. Even more surprising, as Sue was quick to point out, were the postal donations from private individuals – everything from five to five hundred pounds each with a note expressing appreciation and support for Sue's initiative. Sue responded by producing a standard letter of thanks which she individualised to each donor. This tended to occupy a large part of every Friday afternoon, when she produced a summary of the week's progress for the principal donors.

Susanne's week settled down with mornings at the gallery and afternoons at the centre. She had asked Douglas to act as chairman on the understanding that if he was unable to take the chair she would deputise for him. A summary of the business was circulated, and matters for action allocated.

Sue knew the importance of keeping the Foundation in the public eye and then realised that they were missing a trick. At the mid-afternoon tea break, she went along to the staffroom and floated her idea to the dozen or so colleagues who were gathered there.

'I have an idea you might like to think about.' The staff looked at her expectantly and one of the retired builders quipped, 'Only one, Sue?'

'Why don't we invite any young unemployed to help us with the decoration? There's a heck of a lot to be done if we're to open in January. It would also be a useful way of judging how attractive this whole enterprise is in the minds of young people. A gentle nudge, if you like, towards getting them into the work ethos. What do you think?'

While Sue was selling her plan to the staff, Monty was in his bedroom trying to construct a letter to Morgan Fairchild and finding it more difficult than he imagined.

Dear Miss Fairchild,

I am young and unemployed. I watched last Sunday's broadcast on TV of BBC Gloucestershire's relayed programme Facing the Future. When Miss Mortimer invited questions from the audience, I was very surprised by the way you criticised her. It seemed to me that everything she is hoping to do is just what is needed in Gloucester right now.

Then I saw your picture in the newspaper the following day and I noticed how unhappy you looked, which made me wonder what Miss Mortimer had said that upset you so much. If you are unhappy, you should talk to someone you can trust who has wide experience of life, otherwise you may become bitter and that ends up hurting you and spoils the enjoyment that life can offer.

I hope my writing to you doesn't make you angry. At the very least you could ask Miss Mortimer if she would be willing to meet you. If you want to reply to this letter, you can leave it at the Camelot Centre. If you wonder how my letter reached you, I gave it to the police because they aren't allowed to give me your address.

Yours sincerely

Mandela

When he had finished writing, he read the letter through two or three times and decided to show it to Sue and then to his parents and hope that it would meet with their approval. He knew they were still angry about the encounter between Cecilia and Miss Fairchild.

Back at the Centre, Sue's proposal to recruit young people to assist with the decoration of the centre was greeted with enthusiasm, and was broadcast at regular intervals over the weekend with the advice to wear old clothes, although protective clothing would be issued.

There would be sandwiches and hot drinks provided at lunchtime and refreshment breaks in the morning and afternoon. Volunteers were asked to be at the training centre at nine o'clock on Monday morning.

✦ ✦ ✦

Sue arrived home at about six o'clock on Friday evening and sorted through the mail, which had shrunk in volume now that the Centre was open throughout the working week and a regular postal delivery in place. She recognised Monty's handwriting on the envelope and studied the letter he'd printed on his laptop. She appreciated the obvious thought and care he had put into the letter, and wondered what Douglas and Clare's reaction would be. Never one to put off till tomorrow what needed doing today, she rang, and as expected, Clare picked up the phone. 'It's Sue here, Clare. Am I interrupting your evening meal?'

In twenty minutes the answer would be yes, but if you need to see any of the youngsters, I can send them over.'

'That's great. Could you ask Monty to come over, please? I won't keep him for more than a few minutes.' There was a pause at the end of the line as she heard Clare calling Monty's name, then Clare was back. 'He's on his way.'

'Thanks a lot, Clare, he won't be long.'

Susanne threw a coat over her shoulders and walked across the lawn to meet Monty. 'Mum's in the kitchen, so we have the lounge to ourselves. Come along in and don't look so worried – I was very moved by your letter.'

Once they were settled, Monty spoke up, 'I don't mean to sound rude, but it's not you I'm worried about. What do you think Mum and Dad will say?'

Susanne gave a reassuring smile. 'Well, to begin with, they will appreciate that you had the good sense to seek their advice as well as mine before sending the letter. All too often we act first and think of the consequences later. To put your mind at rest, I'm willing to raise the matter with them and assure them that you will not be put in any situation that poses a risk. I know they had a scare over Cecilia, but you are two years older and a sturdy young man for your age, certainly as tall if not taller than Miss Morgan le Fay.

'Rest easy, Monty. If anyone is going to meet her it will be me, since I've been the object of her attention from day one. If you became involved directly and she knew she was dealing with a young teenager, she would smell a rat and you share enough features in common with Cecilia for her to put two and two together. As far as your family is concerned, the buck stops with me, not you.' Monty gave a visible sigh of relief, as if a load had been lifted from his shoulders.

'Your letter is anonymous and could have been written by an 18 year old. She has no way of knowing who you are or where you live, and if your letter gives her pause for thought she will contact me sooner or later. I suggest that when an opportunity arises, the four of us sit down together and see what emerges. Now scoot off home and if your Mum asks what we talked about, say that I'd like to come over when she and your Dad have a minute or two free. Okay?'

After two very demanding weeks, Sue was taken aside by her father after Friday's evening meal while Sarah busied herself in the kitchen. When they were settled in his study, Bob gave her a searching look. 'We need to talk. Your mother and I are immensely proud of everything you've done in such a short time. We know that you have a busy schedule during the next few weeks. I know a doctor is not supposed to treat members of his family, but you must realise that if you insist upon driving yourself at your present pace, without making time to relax, you will almost certainly have a break-down.

'You may feel that you are indispensable, and of course you want to do the best you can. Visit any churchyard and you'll see plenty of memorials to people who in their time thought that the world would not survive without them. All I'm asking is that you pace yourself as much for the sake of the young people you want to help as for your own sake. None of us can burn the candle at both ends and in the middle indefinitely. We just burn out if we're not careful. I want you to protect your weekends and treat them as off-limits to calls from or about the Centre. Do you understand what I am saying?'

'Of course I do, Dad. Thank you for putting things in perspective. I will off-load some of the jobs I've taken on and unless it's a genuine emergency I will follow up any weekend calls on Monday afternoons from now on. It's just that the whole project has expanded far beyond what I expected and people insist upon treating me as the boss when I'm simply a member of the team.'

Her father leant across and planted a kiss on her forehead. 'Mum will be pleased and unless you have a prior engagement, we've reserved tickets at the Theatre Royal Bristol to mark your ring-fenced weekends. By the way, while you were in the bath, Douglas popped over to say that he and Clare are free at nine o'clock. Don't stay up too late, Sweetheart, and have a lie-in tomorrow.'

When Sue tapped on the kitchen door of Briars

Patch, Monty opened it. 'Thanks for coming over,' he whispered. 'I told Mum and Dad you wanted to discuss something concerning me with them. That's all I said.'

'That's fine, Monty,' she replied, 'lead on and let's put them in the picture. I'll start the ball rolling and you can pick it up as we go along.' They moved through into the Willoughbys' lounge with its exposed beams and a wide-breasted open fire crackling merrily.

'It's good to see you, Sue, and I must say we're curious to hear what our son has been up to,' said Clare with a sly chuckle. 'Come and sit down.' Douglas was hovering near the drinks cabinet, but Susanne shook her head, 'It's very kind of you, but I tend not to drink after the evening meal, and I'll be with the fairies soon enough when my head hits the pillow.'

When they were settled, Sue explained the purpose of her visit. 'As everyone knows, I was on the receiving end of some rather bitter comments from Morgan Fairchild last Sunday evening until Andy Powell stepped in. The TV coverage and the papers made rather a lot of her intervention and published an unflattering picture of her for good measure. I received a lot of reassurance from the BBC staff as well as the studio audience, which wasn't picked up in the broadcast itself. But Monty was quite upset and talked to me about it the following day, and made a suggestion which we both agreed you should know about. Right, Monty, it's over to you.'

Monty looked a trifle nervous and then produced two copies of the draft letter and handed them to his parents. 'Do you think I should send this letter, Dad?' His father studied the letter closely and then Clare spoke to Sue, 'What was your reaction when you read the letter?'

'Before I answer that, Clare, I must make it clear there is no way I would put Monty at any risk on my account. I'm not in the business of hiding behind children – especially these children that I love so much. That's why we both needed to share it with you. The reality is that Morgan Fairchild has formed an intense dislike of me and she's already made herself very unpopular with the police. Monty pointed out to me how unhappy she looks and feels driven to increasingly desperate measures that recoil upon her own head. I think Monty has a point. It may be that a conciliatory approach is a better way of resolving the issues that trouble her. I don't want Monty to do anything that goes against your judgment. If the letter is sent, I see no way in which she can identify the sender. She will not think it's the work of a thirteen year old schoolboy. I saw it before supper for the first time and it seemed the kind of letter a young, unemployed 18 year old might well have written, not your dear, thoughtful Monty.

'The two things we don't know are whether she will reply and, if she does, what her response will be. The decision is clearly one that you have to make and Monty quite sensibly will abide by what you decide.'

Douglas tousled his son's hair. 'Monty, you need to know that adults sometimes think that they have all the answers. A knee-jerk reaction is to let Miss Fairchild stew in her own juice, and that could be a very dangerous course to adopt. Like you, I was disturbed by her outburst; Sue didn't deserve to be treated so shabbily. But you have pointed to what we all ought to have noticed: a very unhappy woman. I don't know what your mother thinks, but I am inclined to say you should send the letter. Who knows, it may be the olive branch she needs. What do you think, Clare?'

'If we can protect Monty's identity and Sue is able to reach some kind of understanding with Morgan Fairchild, I agree with you that Monty can send the letter. How will it be delivered, Sue?'

'Either Bryan Holden or Jackie Wilson, who have been a marvellous support, will see it gets there, and they won't know who the author is, either. That information stays between the four of us. No-one else needs to know. If she replies, I'll see the letter first, because all Centre mail comes to me first, before it goes to a particular department, unless it is addressed

148

by name to a Trustee or staff member.'

The weekend appeal resulted in twenty-eight young volunteers waiting at the ground floor entrance to the Camelot building at nine o'clock on Monday morning. They were issued with overalls, protective goggles and papier-mâché mob caps. Divided into twelve pairs, each pair was made responsible to a staff supervisor for the decoration of two units. The four who were not painting were detailed to sweep, clean and remove any splashes of emulsion paint. The emphasis was on light, bright pastel colours with an obliterating white primer. The cleaning detail replenished the paint trays and rinsed out the rollers when necessary. Meanwhile, the supervisors concentrated on the undercoating and painting of doors and window frames prior to gloss coating once the walls had been finished.

Hot drinks were served at eleven o'clock and again at mid-afternoon. There was a one hour lunch break at one o'clock when sandwiches were served and a choice of drinks available. Clear risk assessment had been carried out and any kind of irresponsible behaviour was nipped in the bud with a verbal warning that their services would no longer be required if there was a repetition. Some of the volunteers had brought radios, which engaged their attention as they began work. The numbers remained steady throughout the week and a positive atmosphere was evident amongst the working parties around the building. Smoking was off limits, and anyone wishing to do so had to wait for the tea breaks or lunch hour and go outside the building.

On Wednesday afternoon, when Susanne arrived at the centre and checked her mail, she noticed a letter addressed to Mandela and popped it straight into her shoulder bag, wondering about its contents. While much of Sue's time was taken up with working through each department's budget for essential start-up costs and the placing of equipment orders, she had a further priority. She kept the mid-afternoon tea break clear to allow her time to join the young volunteers and discover what thoughts they had about future employment plans. It was evident from the conversations she had that the volunteers regarded their time at Camelot as an opportunity to gauge its usefulness in getting into work. About half were last summer's school leavers, while the rest had either been unable to find work or been in and out of temporary employment at the unskilled end of the job market. Sue anticipated that they would be among the first to apply for a place on one of the centre's courses.

When she returned to her office, she began to draft the application form directed at the eighteen to twenty-five age group who had been unemployed for at least six months. The form, when it was printed and distributed to the city's job centre and public library, would need to be completed and returned by Monday 7 December. Successful applicants would be notified by Monday 21 and the Camelot Foundation Training Centre would open its doors to the first intake of students on Monday 4 January. There would be four eleven-week terms, with a week's holiday at the end of term one, three weeks' holiday at the end of terms two and three, and a week's holiday at the end of the course before a new enrolment in the following year. Applicants would be required to accept and sign up to the following conditions:

Repeated absenteeism and/or unsatisfactory time-keeping will lead to expulsion unless good reason can be demonstrated.

The same sanction will be applied without any prior warning to those found in possession of illegal substances while on the premises.

Disruptive behaviour will likewise lead to expulsion after one verbal warning.

A no-smoking policy will be enforced within the building. Smoking will be permitted only in the break periods and outside the building.

Smoke alarms will be fitted in all the toilet blocks.

Sue believed it was important to have clear boundaries regarding unacceptable behaviour and to enforce it from day one.

By the time she had produced a coherent application form and Notes for Your Information it was time to think about going home. She passed her draft to one of the IT volunteers who had opted to work in the admin department once the painting had been completed, and asked her to photocopy the draft and place copies in all the staff pigeon holes. Ten minutes later, she was weaving her way through the busy traffic. As she arrived at her home, she remembered the letter that Monty would be expecting and went and posted it through the Willoughbys' mail box. She wondered what Morgan had to say for herself, then hurried across to open the gate and drive in and then close the gate behind her. Doubtless Monty would check to see if there was any letter for him as soon as he noticed her car parked in the drive.

Susanne had just had a shower and was getting dressed when her mother called to her. 'You've a visitor and I've suggested he makes himself comfortable in the lounge.' Sue put a brush through her hair and then hurried downstairs to find Monty flicking through the weekend colour supplements. He jumped up as soon as she walked through the door.

Chapter Eleven
LET HEALING BEGIN

'It's arrived! The reply from Miss Fairchild.' He handed it to her. Sue closed the door behind her and settled in her favourite fireside chair to read the letter.

Dear Mandela,

I am sure that is not your real name, but you are the first person who has shown me any kindness or consideration since I came to Gloucestershire a few weeks ago. I am afraid I've been around too long to imagine that there's anything you can do for me.

A long time ago when I was very young someone hurt my mother and my family life was turned upside down. The person who was responsible for all this had no idea how my life was ruined. All he cared about was his own son, whom he then took away from my mother soon after she had given birth. The child was hidden away for fifteen years, supposedly for his safety. My mother pined for him and I felt she no longer cared for me in the way she used to do.

Ever since then I have felt that I don't matter to anyone. As for Miss Mortimer, she is part of the problem in ways I cannot explain to you. Perhaps one day I may get to meet her. For now, thank you for your letter, and No, I am not angry. I hope you soon get a job.

Morgan Fairchild

Susanne returned the letter to Monty. 'You were right and I was wrong in taking so much notice of Merlin's warnings that they clouded my judgment. If it's not too late, I must try and put things right between us. Show the letter to your Mum and Dad. I'll contact Morgan straight away and see if we can arrange to meet. Thank you, again, for being a peace-maker.' She gave him a warm hug as he stood up to leave and pretended not to notice the pink flush on his face as they left the room.

When Monty had gone, Sue flicked through the Gloucester telephone directory. She found the entry she was looking for: Piper O, Homelea, Albert Road,

Cheltenham. She dialled the number. 'Good evening, is it possible for me to speak to Miss Fairchild, please? I know this is when most people are having their evening meal, but it is a matter of some importance.'

'She is in. I'll give her a call. Who shall I say wishes to speak to her?'

'Susanne Mortimer. I think she'll know who I am.'

'Oh yes, I'm sure she'll know. I hope she's not in any trouble. Just wait, Miss Mortimer, while I call her.' Susanne could hear a muffled conversation and then the sound of someone hurrying down a flight of stairs. The phone was picked up.

'Hello, Morgan. We didn't get much opportunity to talk the last time we saw each other. I think it's about time we met, and probably the sooner the better for both of us, before the whole business descends into farce. What about meeting up for coffee or a lunch-time snack, my treat? I suggest the Eastgate shopping centre, the West Mall on the mezzanine floor where the fast food bars and coffee shops are located.'

There was a short silence at the other end of the line. 'Why have you suddenly changed your tune? Are you going to try and make a fool of me again?'

Sue resisted the temptation to point out that Morgan was the author of her own misfortunes. 'No, I'm not doing anything of the sort. I just want us to stop playing games to see who blinks first. We need to have a sensible and serious talk in a place where no-one will take a blind bit of notice of two young women engaged in conversation. It's clear there are things you want to know and I would rather we did our talking in a civilised manner. I spend afternoons at the training centre and apart from Mondays and Fridays when I have a working lunch on site, I can meet you at twelve-thirty any other week day. I can't stay longer than an hour, but what can't be said in an hour probably isn't worth saying anyway.'

'When were you thinking of having this meeting?'

'You decide. Today's Wednesday, and I can manage tomorrow, otherwise it will have to be next week.'

'Let's make it tomorrow, then.'

'That's fine, Morgan. I'll look forward to meeting you.'

'Thank you for ringing. Goodbye.' The dialling tone kicked in and Sue replaced the receiver. Suddenly, for no apparent reason, she felt a great burden of anxiety taken off her and hoped that it was not false optimism. She put a quick call through to the Willoughby household to let them know that she had fixed up a lunch date with Morgan the following day.

Susanne made good time from Cheltenham to Gloucester through the lunch-time traffic and secured a table for two where she studied the choice of Lite Bites on offer. She had placed herself where she could see over the balcony to the ground floor shopping mall, and shortly before twelve-thirty spotted Morgan moving towards the stairs leading to the mezzanine level. Sue was in her gallery outfit: smart but understated. Jeans and sweater were reserved for the Foundation. She raised an arm as Morgan arrived at the top of the stairs and studied her as she made her way to the table, noting her casual but arty ensemble. Sue stood up and offered her hand in greeting. After a slight hesitation, Morgan responded, and there was brief contact between them.

'Thank you for coming, Morgan. Now, what would you like? I've used this fast-food outlet quite often since taking on the Foundation. The baguettes are fresh and the fillings first-class. Shall I grab us some coffee while you look at the menu card?'

'I'd like a latte plus a tuna and mayo baguette, please.'

'I'll join you in a latte and I'm having a coronation chicken baguette – they're addictive.' She moved off to the counter to place the order and returned with two lattes and brown sugar sachets. 'The baguettes will be about five minutes. Would you like to start,

159

and can we use first names, please?'

Morgan gave a deep sigh and then began speaking. 'Last week I received a letter from someone who described himself as young and unemployed and signed himself Mandela, which was clearly a pseudonym. It was a short letter, but a very kind and thoughtful one, and it carried a punch which quite literally took my breath away. In fact, that night I sobbed my heart out because he made me see myself as he saw me and I didn't like what I saw – a bitter and twisted woman making her life a total misery. For what? Because of something that happened a long time ago.' She took out a handkerchief from her jacket and wiped her eyes. 'When I was still in Cornwall at the beginning of the month, I read the newspaper reports of your sudden disappearance and it was as if someone was walking over my grave. I have a studio there, so I simply locked up and came up here and booked into a local B & B. When you turned up in Gloucester claiming to have lost your memory, I sensed that you could answer questions that I needed to ask. However, I went about it in a stupid way. I antagonised the police on a number of occasions and lost my rag at the BBC studios.

'I wrote back to Mandela and tried to explain my behaviour: a mother deceived and abused; a loving father replaced by a step-father I grew to hate; a half-brother torn from his mother's arms at birth but supplanting me in my mother's affection. Although he was absent, he stood between us and fifteen years later came back to claim his rights. And now I believe that he is about to stalk the land again, and I want to destroy him before he destroys me.' Morgan paused and drank her coffee.

Sue picked up where Morgan had stopped. 'I'm not clear where you think I come into all this. Can you tell me what it is you want to know, Morgan?'

Morgan put her cup down. 'Are you Guinevere, daughter of Leodegrance of Cameliard? Have you been reunited with Arthur Pendragon?' Susanne gave Morgan a disarming smile that was totally free of mockery or amusement.

'I can assure you I am not Guinevere and I have not been reunited with Arthur. But I will tell you something that very few people know. Like you, I have a sad tale to tell which haunts me still. My natural parents abandoned me when I was just a few hours old. They left me at the lodge gate of a convent in Wiltshire that cared for unmarried mothers. I was fostered and eventually adopted by Robert and Sarah Mortimer, who were unable to have children of their own. For the past nineteen years, I have pondered this question: Why was I abandoned? I would like to know who my real parents are. I would like to know whether I will ever meet them.'

'Morgan, we all have ghosts in the closet, but I have tried throughout my life to put aside the questions I cannot answer and be grateful to my adoptive parents, who have showered so much love and care upon me. The rest you heard at the London Road studio.'

For half a minute, Morgan stared at Susanne before she responded. 'Susanne, there is something you should know about yourself. As I live and breathe, you are the absolute spitting image of Guinevere, and Arthur would be the first to recognise that fact.'

'But how can you possibly know that, Morgan?'

'How can I know that? Because I am Morgan le Fay, daughter of the Duke of Cornwall and his wife Igraine. When Arthur became the unquestioned leader of the British, I had occasion to see Guinevere many times.'

'I understand what you are saying, Morgan, but even if I look like Guinevere, I am not that lady, and I would say exactly the same to Arthur if he ever crossed my path. The young man who sent you the letter was telling you no more than the truth. Let go of any thoughts of revenge, or you will call down upon yourself untold misery. You are a very attractive woman, and when you smile or laugh, your beauty lights up any room you enter. It's time to let go of the hurt and the rejection and embrace life.

'I take the view that my natural parents were so young, and so totally unprepared for the responsibilities of parenthood that they did what they thought best. I cannot blame them, and neither can I spend my life worrying or wondering how it might have been otherwise. Once the Camelot Centre is up and running, I will be off to university or wherever life leads me and take the Romans' advice: Carpe diem – seize the day or, as I prefer it, enjoy the day! Isn't that what you should be doing, Morgan?'

Morgan gave another deep sigh. 'But where do I start? I've tended to avoid men's company, but I really did like Bryan Holden, until I blew it.'

'Have you ever thought of making your peace with Arthur?'

Morgan gave a bitter laugh. 'Arthur wouldn't let me get within a hundred miles of him.'

'How can you be so sure?'

'There's been too much blood and bitterness between us. That's hardly a basis upon which to build trust.'

Sue persisted. 'Think about it, anyway, and if you really do like Bryan Holden, I'll put in a good word for you if I see him. Ah! Here come the baguettes. Could we have two more lattes, please?'

The confrontation which Susanne had dreaded turned out to be a healing for both of them, as they saw one another not as enemies, but sharing similar hurtful memories and regrets. When the time came for Susanne to be on her way, they agreed to meet on Thursdays each week to cement what they hoped would be a genuine understanding.

When Susanne gave an account of her lunch date to the three Willoughbys that evening, she reminded Monty not to say anything about his part in the matter to anyone else. 'Morgan's hold on a more normal life is still very fragile, and I'm hoping that the friendship I've offered as a result of your initiative will pay positive dividends in terms of her future happiness. If she ever had a suspicion that we had engineered it between us, it would all fall apart, of that I am sure. She would see it as pity, not love. You do understand?' Monty's reply was quite decisive. 'Of course I do! I wouldn't dream of hurting her.'

✦ ✦ ✦

By the end of the last week in November, the interior decoration had been completed and the young volunteers were treated to a hot lunch to express appreciation for their hard work. They were given advance copies of a leaflet detailing the courses being offered, the conditions attached to being accepted for training and an application form. During her mid-afternoon encounters with them, Susanne recognised that many of them hoped to be considered for the January intake.

The common reaction, when talking with them, was that the prospect of gaining some basic skills was preferable to lying in bed half the day watching television or drifting around the city centre with nothing to do after checking at the job centre for casual employment vacancies. In the first week of December, completed applications began to arrive by every post. From the start of the project, Sue had given a lot of thought to the staff-student ratio, and came to the conclusion that Professor Schumacher had the right answer when he said, 'Small is beautiful'. The availability of so many staff volunteers meant that she argued for a class size limited to twenty and two staff members working in partnership to reinforce each other's skills, supervise the practical implications of the course work and maintain discipline.

December saw also the arrival of the centre's furniture, specialised equipment and the installation of departmental hardware, whether for the hairdressing salon, the IT facility, the catering area or the ground floor building and auto engineering workshops. Gradually, everything began to come together. One important asset was that each of the upper floors had its own Victorian steel gantry which provided access to the building. The gantries had been load-tested to their design limits and signed off by the industrial inspector from the Health and Safety authorities. Each floor was allocated its reception day for delivery and the passage of low-loaders, box body vans and flat-bed trucks was complemented by a supply of pallets and two medium-sized fork-lift trucks loaned by a local building company. The centre was on the up and up; soon it would be running.

Susanne was working through a pile of applications before passing them to the departmental staff for their assessment when there was a tap at the door. 'Come in.'

Bryan Holden opened the door. 'Am I interrupting?'

'Come on in, Bryan, and take a seat.' She pushed the papers to one side, 'Is this an official visit?'

'Not really. I wanted to thank you for putting me in the picture about Morgan. In fact, I'd quite like to draw a line under everything that's come between us. You see, Sue, I like the lady, I like her a lot.'

'Oh Bryan, that's wonderful and just what she needs. Some TLC will do wonders for her, especially from someone who is honest and trustworthy. I wish you well.'

Bryan gave her a shy grin, 'I just thought I'd run the idea past you. I'll let you get back to work.'

✦   ✦   ✦

Morgan was channel-hopping after the early evening news on Friday when Olive Piper called up the stairs, 'Telephone call for you, Morgan.'

'Thanks, I'm on my way down.' She went into the guests' lounge and closed the door behind her and picked up the phone. 'Morgan Fairchild.'

'Hello, Morgan. It's Bryan Holden.'

'Oh! What have I done now?'

'Nothing. This is not an official call, but a personal one to ask how you are and whether you'd like to go out this evening and see a film.'

'Are you asking me out on a date?'

'I suppose I am. Does that surprise you?'

'You've been talking to Susanne Mortimer, haven't you?'

'Considering the station is just round the corner from Camelot, that's not unusual. We sometimes see each other at the fast food bar, especially on Mondays and Fridays when she has to be at the centre for committee meetings. But you haven't answered my question – would you like to go out?'

'Give me one good reason why I should.'

'You may not believe me, but despite all the issues that have muddied the waters in the past few weeks, I actually like you and I thought it might be a good idea to get to know you better. The cinema is a good place to be together, enjoy a shared experience and not feel obliged to do any more than that. I'll see you safely home and then go back to my pad. What follows thereafter we don't need to know tonight. Let's just go with the flow.'

'Fair enough. It's not the chat-up line most men would try, but Yes, I would enjoy an evening out. When should I expect you to be here?'

'Thirty seconds. I'm sitting in my car outside your front door. Wrap up well, it's quite cold with a sharp frost forecast for tonight.'

Morgan hurried back upstairs, grabbed her winter coat, matching beret and scarf. She flew downstairs, checked herself in the hall mirror, shrugged and quietly closed the front door behind her. Bryan was standing by the passenger door and she slipped into the seat. 'Thank you, it's a nice surprise. Which cinema are we bound for?'

'It's in the Gloucester Docks area. A small building but listed and therefore protected from demolition and redevelopment. The ground floor houses the foyer, bar, lounge and toilet facilities. The upper floor has been converted into a hundred-seater, raked auditorium using the latest digital projection system, thanks to a millennium grant. We aim to show one film a month and have a mix of recent releases and back titles that have been formatted to DVD, which enables us to have regular short season runs. During this last quarter of the year we're featuring Anthony Hopkins. Tonight's film is *Meet Joe Black.*

'I was worried for a moment. I thought it might be *The Silence of the Lambs.*

'No, we don't show eighteen category films. They're not family friendly. We have a core membership of one hundred, so there's always a waiting list, but seats allowing we can bring guests. Because everyone involved with the centre works on a voluntary basis, and because it's regarded as a civic amenity run on a not-for-profit basis, we've been able to be registered as a charity. But what about you, when you're in Cornwall?'

In the darkness of the car and the unforced communication with Bryan, Morgan felt herself relaxing in much the same way as she had during her lunch date with Susanne the previous day.

'My base is at Clovelly and I'm part of what's known as the Artists' Colony. The subject matter in Cornwall is so varied; the light is fantastic if you're into water colours. I do quite a lot of scenic views which holiday visitors seem to appreciate. I also dabble in acrylics and tote my gear to special places that have a real sense of atmosphere: the old tin mines, rocky outcrops, quaint villages with narrow streets. You should come down and see for yourself.'

'I'd like that, Morgan.' Bryan left it hanging in the air between them. It was just after seven o'clock when they arrived at The Cabin. Bryan parked his car and took Morgan's arm to guide her in the sparsely lighted area that led to the little cinema. Inside, a substantial number of people had already arrived. Bryan produced his season ticket and bought a guest ticket for Morgan. 'Can I get you a drink, while you find us a table? We're licensed for wine but not spirits, the beer comes in cans and there's the usual range of soft drinks.'

'A glass of medium white would be lovely, thank you.'

Settled at a table for two, Bryan nodded greetings to fellow members who caught his eye.

'You use the word 'we' quite a lot when talking about the cinema. Were you involved in the conversion?'

'Very much so. There was an appeal for volunteers posted in the library and the local pubs and clubs, followed by the usual public meeting. Then a working party was set up and was able to draw together enough people with practical skills to do a decent job of converting the building, starting with the upper floor, and then down here so that we didn't carry rubbish or wet paint upstairs and spoil all the hard work. The walls had to be covered with sound-absorbent material so that the speaker system didn't create an echo. It was much like the Camelot project, but obviously on a smaller scale.'

At that moment a warning bell sounded. 'That's the five minute bell, so we'd better go and claim our seats. If you need the ladies' room, it's at the far end of the lounge and clearly signed.' After the customary safety announcement, the house lights were dimmed; the buzz of conversation died down. They were about to Meet Joe Black. Morgan's hands were resting in her lap until Bryan took her left hand and held it lightly in his right hand. Morgan resisted the temptation to remove her hand and gave herself up to enjoying the film and being with Bryan. He whispered in her ear, 'The critics panned the film when it was released. You make up your own mind.'

She whispered back, 'I will' and pressed his hand as if to confirm her reply.

When the film ended, they followed the crowd back to the car park, arm in arm. The journey back to Cheltenham seemed to last no more than a few minutes, as they discussed the film. Morgan was quite firm in her opinion: 'I think the critics were wrong.' At Homelea, Bryan opened the passenger door. As they stood together, Morgan shivered. It was as cold as Bryan had predicted, but the shiver had nothing to do with the night air. Bryan took Morgan's hands in his own. 'Thank you for saying Yes – I have really enjoyed being with you.' Morgan looked up at him and took him by surprise, 'Would you like to kiss me, Bryan?'

'If you mean a kiss on the cheek, then No, I wouldn't. If it's on the lips, the answer's Yes.'

She stretched up and kissed him on the lips. They stood, locked in each other's arms. 'Thank you, Bryan. You are a good man and I want to get to know you better, too.'

He released her. She blew him a final kiss as she let herself into the guest house.

Chapter Twelve

BEHOLD CAMELOT

Acting upon her father's advice, Susanne had a late breakfast on Saturday and after a brisk walk to the church and back, settled down with the morning papers. She congratulated herself on keeping the weekend clear. Even as she reflected on the fact, the phone rang and she groaned inwardly. Since her parents were in Charlton Kings to return library books and pick up some fresh vegetables and sundry bits of shopping, she picked up the phone. 'Susanne Mortimer here.'

'Oh hi, Sue. It's Bryan. I thought I'd give you an update on Morgan. I'm ringing from the station.'

'I hope you aren't going to give me any bad news.'

'Not at all – quite the reverse. The Willoughbys

have notified us that they do not wish to pursue the incident involving Cecilia, and Morgan wrote a letter of apology which she dropped off at the studios yesterday morning. The BBC is taking no further action in the matter. We've tracked down a dodgy second-hand car dealer in Penzance who may be facing charges of handling stolen vehicles, which should make things easier for Morgan. She has been bound over to keep the peace and her driving licence has been returned with three penalty points for infringing traffic regulations. I suppose you could say she's been released into my custody.' This was said with a light chuckle. 'What's more, I took the bull by the horns and asked her out last night. She accepted and we drove to the Cabin Cinema in Gloucester Docks and I think she really enjoyed the evening. I know that I did.'

'Oh Bryan, you are a treasure! I sense that she finds it difficult to trust men and I'm certain you're just the man she needs in her life. She's a lonely soul, but she needs someone to love. I think you could be good for one another. Will you stay in the police?'

'It's early days, but I think so. I had twelve years in the army but the postings created problems, including a broken engagement because another guy who fancied my fiancée was available while I was getting shot at in Iraq. It's a story as old as the hills. I've passed the exam for promotion to sergeant, but have to wait until there's a vacancy. If Morgan wants us to make a life together, we'll have to decide whether that vacancy should be in Cornwall or Gloucester. I guess we'll take one step at a time. Enjoy your weekend, and thanks again for putting me in touch with Morgan.'

On Sunday, Sarah and Susanne spent the afternoon putting up decorations and freshly cut holly in the lounge and hall. The Christmas holly wreath was suspended from a hook in the front porch, and when the Christmas tree had its full complement of baubles and fairy lights, Sarah sat down. 'I think we've earned ourselves a well-deserved cup of tea, don't you?'

'Absolutely, Mum. You stay put and I'll go and make the tea for a change.' Before Sarah could respond, Sue was already through the lounge door heading for the kitchen. Five minutes later, she appeared with the laden tea trolley and a tin of assorted biscuits.

'Thank you, darling.' Susanne gave the tea a quick stir, then poured her mother a cup and invited her to help herself to biscuits. When they were both settled, Sarah lost no time in opening a conversation.

'When will you be winding down at the training centre? You are looking quite tired.'

'We have our final meeting tomorrow afternoon to check the applications and double-check all the departments are ready to open up shop on the first

Monday in January. After that, we'll be heading home for the holiday and the recharging of batteries. I will be back to my normal hours at the gallery, which closes for a week at lunchtime on Christmas Eve. Barring unforeseen problems, once the courses get started, I shouldn't have anything like the demands of the past two months, so I hope to take a back seat and leave it to the professionals.'

Sarah's face brightened. I think you're very sensible to take that approach. Your father and I have been quite concerned about the heavy responsibility you took on, and there were times when we wondered if you might sink under the weight of it all. I gather that Miss Fairchild is no longer making a nuisance of herself. That was something you didn't need.'

Sue sensed that her mother was fishing, and was more than a little curious about Morgan. 'I took advice and decided we needed to sort things out between us. We both had some baggage to deal with, and now have a better understanding of one another. We meet for lunch once a week and she has a nice boyfriend, which makes her a very happy bunny. I don't think she'll be a problem in the future.'

Sarah's agenda was not complete. 'And what about you? If you're working yourself out of a job at the centre, have you any idea what you will do long-term?'

'I have a place to do a fine arts degree at Durham,

but I'm wondering whether I should think of a course at a university nearer home. I must do some digging around during the next couple of weeks. The gallery is happy to keep me on but the work doesn't stretch me, and I think I need the application and discipline of a degree course to master the subject more fully.'

Sarah nodded her approval. 'So long as you don't wear yourself out in the meantime, and miss the opportunity to make the best use of your ability, I'm sure it will all come together.'

'Thanks, Mum, I hope so too.'

On Monday afternoon, with just ten days to Christmas, the committee met for the last time before the centre opened its doors in the New Year. All the courses were full and a reserve list drawn up should anyone drop out at the last minute. Sue expressed the hope that the students would make the best possible use of the courses they were taking and that the staff would feel a sense of achievement once the programme got underway.

'And talking of way, there are ways in which we can help the students to help themselves and the centre at the same time. Let me give you a couple of examples.

'Once you are persuaded that those who are training to become hairdressers or barbers have reached a satisfactory standard, I see no reason why they should not offer to cut and blow-dry fellow students' hair at training rates. If a charge of five pounds is levied, half can be kept by the trainee and half ploughed back into the salon training fund. In the same way, once the catering students have shown they can produce an appetising hot lunch, the same principle can apply: half the money goes into a common pot which is divided equally amongst those who prepared the food and half builds up the catering account. Meanwhile, the students get their lunch at subsidised prices. We need to demonstrate to those who have given us financial support that we believe in self-help – everybody wins. But, and this is important, if we decide to go down that road, it must be confined to the centre. We are not about to undercut those whose livelihood depends on what our students are learning to do by inviting members of the public onto the premises. This is purely and simply domestic housekeeping, which applies to staff as well as students.

'There's just one more matter I need to raise. No-one is indispensable, and I shall not be here forever. It has always been my intention to further my interest by pursuing a fine arts degree, and I hope to start my programme at the commencement of the new academic year next October if I can persuade a department to accept me. I will be here until the end of September, by which time the Camelot Centre should be a going concern and with the staff we have recruited, I'm sure that is precisely what will happen.'

✦   ✦   ✦

When Sue finally left the centre on Monday evening, the prospect of almost three weeks' break before she was caught up in the launch of the Centre was tempered by the knowledge that she would be working at the gallery full-time for seven of those days. In reality she would have barely two weeks to call her own. Three days later, Sue and Morgan met for their Thursday lunch in Cheltenham, since the Centre was closed and Sue was working her normal shift. While they were waiting for their order, Morgan asked a question, 'One thing has puzzled me since our first lunch date. You seemed to accept quite naturally that I could have known Guinevere. Why were you so ready to believe me?'

Susanne did not seem the least bit troubled. 'I wondered when you might pick that up, and I guess now is as good a time as any to explain my reaction. From the time I arrived back home, I could not help being aware (please excuse what I'm going to say) of your almost obsessive determination to know what really happened when I went missing. At that time I had been given good reason to be wary of you and what you might do to me. If you had been in my position, I think you would have reacted in much the same way as I did.

'However, there was one thing I could not get my head round. How did I come to sleep for such a long time? Why did I have no idea of who I was or where I lived? Christine Simpson, who gave me a thorough physical examination, found no sign of any kind of injury or interference. Mild hypothermia was the extent of my state of health at that time. During those four days when I was 'out of it', I had some kind of dream in which I was visited by an old man who claimed to know me. He said he was looking for Arthur and that when he found him, Arthur would need me. He also repeatedly told me to beware of Morgan le Fay, who would cause me trouble.

'By Friday afternoon, after having taken in food and a great deal to drink, and after the initial shock of being re-united with my father, I quickly readjusted to my home surroundings. So when you told me I was unmistakably Guinevere, I realised that the incredible had become reality: Merlin is abroad, Morgan is abroad, Arthur and his companions are abroad or perhaps very soon will be. So you can see why I accepted what you told me as being nothing other than the truth.

'I hope you will forgive me for not sharing this

with you when we met for our first lunch. It seemed important at that time that we should come to some degree of trust and I hope that as you and Bryan get to know each other better you will see we are people upon whom you can rely. Speaking of Bryan, how are things working out for you?'

For the first time since she had come to know Morgan, she noticed her blush deeply. 'I know it sounds crazy, but I feel as if he's the person I've been looking for and have found at last. I think he feels the same way about me. We just enjoy being together and Yes, I love him. There, I've said it. He is decent, honest, caring and accepts me as I am. He knows very little about me beyond the fact that I have no family and earn my living as an artist in Cornwall. All we know is that we want to be together, either there or here. And it's you we have to thank for making it happen, so how could I possibly imagine that you would wish me harm?'

On Christmas Eve, last minute shopping for last minute presents occupied Susanne when the gallery closed its doors at one o'clock. She rang Bryan, Morgan, Jackie and Christine to wish them seasonal greetings and joined in the traditional festivities with the midnight service at Dowdeswell Church, Christmas Day at home and a Boxing Day afternoon walk with the Willoughbys.

On New Year's Day, Robert and Sarah hosted a drinks party for friends and neighbours, and before Susanne had caught her breath, it was back to work. Her commitment to the gallery meant that she would not be present at the commencement of the centre's beginning of term welcome, which by common agreement was to be fairly low key.

Douglas Willoughby, as chairman of the committee, sat behind a small rostrum flanked on either side by the trustees and staff members in the large conference room on the top floor. He stood up to address the students. 'I shan't keep you long, but I do want to wish you well as you embark on your chosen course. December seems a long way off when January has only just begun, but if you apply yourselves in these coming months, you will be surprised how many new skills and how much valuable experience you will have gained.

'Your tutors have a vast fund of practical knowledge to share with you. Listen to what they say, seek to imitate what they do and at all times treat them with the respect they deserve. The moving spirit behind the Camelot Centre cannot be with us this morning; she has a job and her employer expects her to earn the salary she receives. She will be here during the afternoons and will want to meet you and get to know you. She is, after all, the same age as most of you.'

'I'd like to share with you the thoughts of someone whose situation at your age was, if anything, worse than yours is likely to be. This is what he has to say about his teenage years, surrounded as he was by poverty and squalor: 'You have to believe in yourself, that's the secret. Even when I was in the orphanage, or when I was roaming the streets trying to find enough to eat, even then I thought of myself as the greatest actor in the world. I had to feel the inner optimism that comes from utter confidence in oneself. Without it, you go down to defeat.'

Douglas paused to let his words sink in. 'He was not mistaken, he was not crazy, he was not kidding himself. He did indeed become one of the world's greatest actors by common consent. His name was on everyone's lips and we who are here this morning stand in a building which shares his initials, for his name was Charlie Chaplin.

'If you wish for success in life, make perseverance your closest friend, let experience be your wise counsellor, make caution your elder brother and hope your guardian and guide. Now go to it, my friends, and show the world what you are made of – and may good fortune be your just reward.'

There was a brief photo shoot to catch the evening

papers, then staff and students dispersed to the departmental work areas and the centre settled down with introductions followed by a brief summary of the ground to be covered in the next four terms. Since the centre was essentially technical in its scope, and a site for a general purpose library problematic, each department carried its own collection of essential reference books appropriate to the course.

When Sue arrived in the afternoon and made a brief tour of the departments, she attracted a great many curious stares, but when the mid-afternoon break bell sounded she sought out a group of students in the dining area and very quickly put them at their ease. 'I'm Susanne Mortimer, but please call me Sue. It's a great joy to see you here and I hope you won't hesitate to let me know if you'd like to talk about your course. My office is on the top floor and if the door is open that means I'm free – if it's closed then I'm talking to another student or a member of staff so you'll have to try again.

'Monday afternoons I'm usually involved with committee meetings to keep this show on the road. On Friday afternoons the door is firmly closed as I work on the weekly report for our financial supporters and the local media. So it's Tuesday, Wednesday or Thursday. Now tell me something about yourselves …'

As the weeks went by, Sue sensed that steady progress was being made, brought about by a combination of the clear practical experience allied to a no-nonsense approach by the staff and the motivation evident amongst the students. She had to hope that by the time this first intake was nearing the end of the year there might be signs of a recovery in the employment market.

There had been early agreement amongst the staff to reject formal written examinations at the end of each term or the end of the year. The work to be covered in four eleven-week sessions could not be put on hold while students took time off to revise. Continuous assessment was the most realistic means of testing, since it would keep the students on their toes knowing every piece of work submitted would count towards their final grade. Many of the staff members recalled the daily spelling test of ten or twenty new words which laid the basis of their command of the English language in their own junior school years.

The other issue concerned the value or otherwise of a 'paper' qualification, given that not all the students enrolled on the centre's registers were academically gifted. Sue felt achievements in practical skills deserved to be acknowledged, and she floated the idea of a Camelot Centre certificate which not only graded practical achievement at class one, two and three levels, but also summarised on the reverse of the certificate the skills gained during the course of the year; skills that a potential employer could put to immediate use.

Meanwhile, a grudging winter finally made way for a spring that ushered in the first promise of a warm summer yet to come. Cold nights were balanced by brilliantly sunny days, which coaxed the students away from the dining area, clutching their baguettes, coffee and fresh fruit, down to the old docks, pairing off in many cases as romances began to bud. Towards the end of the second term, Sue was at home for the late spring bank holiday weekend when the phone rang. It was Lucy at Stonehenge with some news. 'Hi there. The National Trust has an acquisitions department which makes use of the major auction houses around the country for the purchase of items to furnish properties which no longer have the appropriate period furniture that they need. We also use the London auction houses to handle pieces which are surplus to our requirements and may attract a better sale price than a provincial auction house can secure.

'Anyway, I've just seen Christie's most recent catalogue for a sale on Wednesday 16 June of early English and mediaeval weapons, ornaments and jewellery, which includes a selection described as 'The Property of a Nobleman' dating from the late fifth and early sixth centuries. Would you be interested in having a day in London to attend the auction? The Oxford professor we met last year quizzed me about the leading auction houses and I gave him details of three of the London firms. He said he was interested in that period and I wondered whether he might be there.'

All the time Lucy was talking, Sue wondered if this was Merlin's way of telling her that he had found Arthur. Virtually all British and Saxon artefacts of value were either in museums or were known to be in private hands. Lucy repeated her question.

'Sorry, Lucy, I was just thinking that the centre is closed for three weeks from 11 June until 5 July and I can take a day's holiday from the gallery, so the answer is Yes, I'd love to spend the day in London with you. It would be quite a coincidence if the professor is there too. If you can put me up on the Tuesday night, we can catch an early train to Waterloo.' They exchanged other bits of news before ringing off.

Chapter Thirteen

THE INVITATION . . .

Lucy and Susanne caught the first train from Salisbury offering a cheap day return and arrived at Waterloo a few minutes after ten o'clock. They crossed over York Road and made their way along the south Embankment, stopping briefly to watch people entering the capsules of the London Eye before leaving the river beneath them as they ascended the steps to Westminster Bridge. Big Ben struck the quarter as they reached the north side and studied the imposing statue of Boadicea and her two daughters recalling the British Queen's revolt against the might of the Roman Empire.

They negotiated the busy junction with Whitehall and headed towards Birdcage Walk and joined the summer visitors in St James' Park. It was a lovely summer day but they realised time was ticking by as they made their way across the park towards St James' Palace. As they approached The Mall, Susanne halted abruptly. 'Psssst! Look who's crossing over ahead of us. That's the professor, isn't it?'

Lucy saw a group of five people walking over the distinctive salmon pink tarmacadam that never ceased to surprise her whenever she was in this part of London. A young girl of about nine was holding the hand of a tall, well-built man, followed by a couple of teenagers. Ahead of them, leading the way, was an elderly man with a mop of flowing white hair; the professor. 'They must be on the way to Christie's.' Susanne nodded her agreement. 'I wonder who the children are, and who the other man is? The teenage couple look as if they're carrying a picnic hamper between them. They're probably going for a picnic in the park after the sale is over. If you don't mind, Lucy, I'd rather not make myself known to them at present. Perhaps we could sit at the back of the sale room and slip out as soon as their collection has been auctioned off.'

Lucy was surprised at her friend's reaction, but decided she must have her own reasons. 'That's fine by me, but while they're picnicking we'll need to get some lunch too. There are one or two eateries in

Victoria Street that I know of. Good food, well cooked at sensible prices.'

By this time they had reached King Street and with five minutes to spare they took their seats at the back. Despite Susanne's protest about not meeting the professor on this occasion, Lucy noticed that she took a very close interest in his adult companion. She took him to be in his early thirties. Sue was wearing her favourite colour, which was a cream, lightweight summer dress, setting off her chestnut hair and this attracted the attention of the teenage girl who was sitting alongside the professor's companion. Momentarily, the girl's eyes met Susanne's, then both of them looked away.

Interest in the sale room was heightened when bidding began for "The Property of a Nobleman", and as the last item in the lot went under the hammer, Sue quickly left her seat, followed by Lucy. Neither of them was aware that the young teenager had noticed their abrupt departure. They made their way to Victoria Street and sat chatting together over lunch. Lucy looked at her friend, 'Jennifer, what is it with you and the professor?'

Susanne sat bolt upright – 'Why do you call me Jennifer?'

Lucy was nonplussed. 'When you joined the work camp in Cornwall at the beginning of your sixth form studies, you registered as Jennifer Mortimer.'

Susanne looked embarrassed and uncomfortable. 'Oh my goodness! I'm so sorry, Lucy. Mum and Dad named me Susanne Jennifer (it's a bit of a long story) and when I was sixteen I asked them why they never made any reference to my second Christian name. It was almost as if I only had one. We didn't exactly fall out, but I did get a bit bolshie over the issue and for almost a year insisted my school friends call me Jennifer until I realised I was being rather stupid and reverted back to Susanne.' She gave Lucy a rather sheepish grin.

Lucy smiled. 'Well, I'm glad we've got that sorted out. Anyway, it's a pity to waste the sunshine, so how about a stroll in the park before we head for home.' They walked back and were crossing the lake via a small bridge when Susanne saw the picnic party – 'Look!'

'Why don't you say Hello to them?'

'No, but I must find out the professor's name.'

Lucy shook her head. 'I thought you knew him. You were as thick as thieves at Stonehenge.'

'I do know him, but I don't know his name or where he lives. Can't you think of some way of finding out? I'll see you by the Guards' Memorial in ten minutes.' Susanne turned back and began walking towards Horse Guards' Parade.

Lucy took a deep breath and approached the small group, who were busy packing the hamper with the cups, plates and plastic cutlery while the little girl was feeding the ducks and pigeons. Within two minutes of greeting the group, Lucy had established that the professor's name was Meriden, but he was not disposed to supply any other information beyond the fact that he lived in Oxford, which Lucy already knew. She gave them her brightest smile and then hurried away. The teenage girl, Sophie, for that was her name, said to the professor as they watched Lucy walk away, 'She was at Christie's this morning with a younger woman … I think she wanted to find out who you were.'

While Sophie was explaining what she had noticed in Christie's auction room, Lucy had rejoined Susanne. 'Well, Susanne, our mystery professor is called Meriden. He lives in Oxford and there is no reason to doubt that he is professor of mediaeval history, which the English Heritage staff at Stonehenge told me at the time of his visit. Once we're back on the train to Salisbury, you can explain what all this is about.' As the train pulled out of Waterloo, Lucy looked keenly at Sue and said, 'Now, Susanne Mortimer, what's this with you and Professor Meriden?'

'He approached me and wanted to know where I had been during the days I went missing. I said it was some kind of box tomb a mile or so from Dorstone.

He immediately identified it as Arthur's Stone, and indicated that he was examining the various sites associated with Arthur, especially where encounters with the Saxons led to decisive battles. More than that, I can't say, because he has been very inconsistent in keeping in touch. I need to know which college he's linked with and ideally a contact address in Oxford so that if he can't be bothered to keep in touch with me, at least I can keep in touch with him – so if you can track him down I'd be very grateful. Meanwhile, thank you for suggesting today's outing. It's been quite an education.'

A few days later, Lucy left a message on the Mortimers' phone and reported the results of her enquiries: 'Professor M Meriden is a Fellow of Magdalen College and being a bachelor lives in college. If he has a private telephone, it is ex-directory. However, he's not in residence at the present time, but said to be living in Dorset. But that information is confidential. Letters addressed to him at Oxford will be forwarded. I hope that is some help and will enable you to track him down.'

Sue wrote a short note to Merlin asking whether Arthur still needed to see her, and signed herself Susanne. Ten weeks later she received a reply postmarked Southampton but notepaper headed Magdalen College, Oxford:

Dear Jennifer,

Since we last met, affairs have moved on apace, as I am sure you will appreciate. Arthur and his companions are settled here in Dorset (address attached below) and he is anxious to see you. There is much to discuss and decide, but I feel certain that when you meet, it should be a private matter between you and Arthur, without my being present. I understand the misgivings you expressed during our brief meeting at the Stone Circle, and feel it would be wrong for me to intrude upon what you need to say to one another.

Be assured that Arthur is very sensitive to the concerns you have, and I have made no attempt to speak for you, as I am well aware you are more than capable of speaking for yourself. Therefore make haste to join us and by all means bring a friend to act as chaperone while you are in the company of thirty men. Perhaps Lucy would be willing to accompany you. The Lodge is a trifle spartan, but we have an excellent housekeeper and the beds are passing fair. Please phone when you can see your way to joining us at Kingston Lodge, Winterborne Kingston, Wimborne, Dorset.

With affection and respect,

Merlin.

As soon as Sue had digested the contents of Merlin's letter, she realised she could not ask Lucy to accompany her without compromising the anonymity that Merlin insisted Arthur and his friends needed. Nevertheless, she knew it was important to her as well as to Merlin and Arthur to take a female companion if at all possible. Morgan could not accompany her, which meant there was just one person she could call on, if she would agree – Lydia.

Lydia would turn sixteen in September; Sue had her twentieth birthday in March. And so she decided to sound out her young friend and if she was reluctant, Sue would not press her on the matter, but travel to Kingston Lodge on her own. Having made up her mind, she rang the Willoughbys and asked if she could speak to Lydia. When Lydia picked up the phone, Sue enquired whether she was busy. 'Not at all. I'm enjoying doing nothing much in particular. I've had my exam results, which weren't at all bad. Monty and I have been whacking tennis balls back and forth on our DIY court. Is there something you want?'

'Let's just say, something's come up which I need to talk over with you. Can we go for a half-hour stroll?'

'This sounds exciting. I'll just let Mum know, then I'll be over in a minute or two.'

The phone clicked and the dialling tone returned. Sue went through to the garden where her mother was dead-heading the few remaining flowering roses. 'Lydia and I are going for a walk. We'll be back in about half an hour. Okay?'

Sarah smiled. 'That'll be nice for both of you. Give her my love.'

Sue waved, 'Will do, Mum.' She made her way round to the drive and spotted Lydia cutting across the lawn to meet her. Susanne greeted her with a high five. 'You're probably wondering what this is all about. I'll tell you once we're out of earshot.'

They walked down the drive and when the gate was closed behind them, Sue produced the letter and invited Lydia to read it as they strolled along.

'Have you told Lucy about this?' Lydia said, as she handed the letter back.

'No, I haven't, and I don't think I can tell her. No-one knows anything about Arthur except the four of us, and I did promise Merlin not to tell anyone else. Let's face it, who would believe us anyway? The only person we've mentioned is the professor. As you can see, he is anxious I should take someone with me. It will be for the inside of one day or an overnight visit at the most. It's a lot to ask, but I wondered whether you would be willing to come with me. Winterborne Kingston is about an hour further on from Stonehenge and I can borrow Dad's sat nav to work out the best route. What do you think?'

They walked on in silence as Lydia pondered Sue's proposal. 'What do I tell Mum and Dad?'

'As much as they need to know. That we met Professor Meriden at Stonehenge last November, that he's professor of mediaeval history at Magdalen College, Oxford, and is on holiday at Winterborne Kingston where his live-in house-keeper looks after the domestic arrangements. He invited me and went on to suggest that I might like to bring a friend for company. You can give them the Dorset address and telephone number. They know you'll be safe with me, and probably regard it as a 'girly' outing. We can't tell them anything about the house, since neither of us has seen it. We'll be sharing a room, and you can say he met Lucy and is known to the staff at Stonehenge. That should be sufficient. In any case, I'm more than happy to ask your parents if they are willing to let you join me on the trip, but leave it to me to explain to Monty and Cecilia why they haven't been included. Any questions?'

'Just one – when do you expect to go?'

'I'd just as soon go next weekend. Leave Saturday morning and if your Mum and Dad are happy about the sleepover, drive home mid-morning on Sunday. With the late Bank Holiday over, the roads shouldn't be so busy the first weekend in September with a new school year about to begin. Are you sure you want to come along?'

Lydia nodded vigorously. 'You bet! It's about time I did something that's not connected with books, besides which, it isn't every day a girl gets to meet King Arthur.' When Lydia raised the subject with Douglas and Clare, they were remarkably relaxed about it. Douglas spoke for both of them, 'Susanne has matured amazingly in the past year; I can't tell you how much responsibility she's carried ever since the Camelot project was launched. However, it's time she thought about her own future. I can see with her close interest in the Renaissance and European culture in general she wants to spend time with an Oxford don who specialises in mediaeval history. I'm sure you'll enjoy the experience, isn't that right, Clare?'

'I couldn't have put it better. Tell Sue we know you'll be safe in her company, and we hope you have a great time, but don't forget to let us know you've arrived safely and when to expect you back home.'

Chapter Fourteen

. . . AND THE RESPONSE

They set off straight after breakfast on Saturday morning, and set the sat nav to get them from Dowdeswell using A roads. When they reached Warminster, they stopped for an eleven o'clock coffee break. From Blandford it was a short run towards Winterborne Kingston. Merlin had given Sue clear directions to Kingston Lodge, and they found themselves with time in hand. To Lydia's surprise, when they reached the Lodge entrance, Sue drove on past and parked the car off the road a few hundred metres further on alongside a farm gate.

'We've twenty minutes to spare before they're expecting us,' Sue explained in response to Lydia's puzzled expression. 'Merlin wants me here to meet

Arthur and I need to put you in the picture as far as I understand it myself. Arthur is expecting to be re-united with his wife, Guinevere (with all that such expectation entails). He expects me to be his wife, which is something I am not able to be. No matter what Merlin says, if Arthur is looking for a wife, he's going to be disappointed. I'm just a twenty-year-old Gloucestershire girl and perhaps I shouldn't have gone along with Merlin's scheme. I didn't ask you to come with me just to be a chaperone to preserve my reputation. I wanted you along because I'm in need of moral support. I hope you don't mind being dragged into this on my account.'

'Oh Sue, I've had my own thoughts about how things might be with you and Arthur. I wouldn't have agreed to making the trip if I hadn't wanted to. It's exciting and I know I'm not the reason for our being here, but I wouldn't have had it any other way. If I can look out for you in the way you've looked out for us all these years, I will have done no more than I ought to do. I'm in your corner; you can count on me.'

'Bless you, Lydia. You don't know how much better that makes me feel. Now let's turn this buggy around and prepare to meet the once and future king.' With that, she switched on the ignition, released the handbrake, performed a neat three-point turn and headed back to Kingston Lodge.

As they turned off the road and entered the Lodge drive, they wondered what kind of reception they would be given. Over to the right as they approached the house, a spacious lawn had been turned into some kind of obstacle course. The gravelled parking area in front of the house itself was deserted, save for one ancient Land Rover parked under a tree to keep the sun off. Susanne began to wonder if they were on a fool's errand, or had mixed up the dates. They felt stiff from the journey and walked over to the entrance of the house with its mock Tudor façade. There was a sturdy bell pull and Sue gave it two vigorous yanks. They could hear it echoing through the house. She was about to ring a second time when they heard footsteps coming along the hall. The door opened and a cheerful middle-aged woman wearing a bright coloured vinyl apron looked at them with a friendly smile. 'Can I help you?'

'We've come to see Professor Meriden by appointment. He should have received a letter from me this week giving our time of arrival, but perhaps the letter went astray.'

'Oh, I'm sorry. You must be Jennifer Cameliard and your friend Lydia. Is that right? I'm afraid we were affected by a local postal dispute and the post has been all over the place this past week. A bundle of letters arrived after they'd all gone out. But my goodness, here I am keeping you standing and forgetting my manners. Do come in.'

She held out her hand, 'I'm Mrs Cooper, the professor's housekeeper. He asked me to make up beds for two young ladies. I hope you won't mind sharing a room. You'll be next to mine. All the others are occupied, I'm afraid.' She led the way into a very large sitting room. 'How far have you travelled?'

'From just the other side of Cheltenham.'

'Oh my dears,' she burst in, 'you must be famished. Why don't you fetch your luggage, and I'll show you your room. If you want to freshen up, there's my bathroom across the landing. The gentlemen don't use it; otherwise they get the sharp edge of my tongue.' She chuckled, with a twinkle in her eye.

Lydia hesitated, and then asked, 'How many gentlemen are staying here, then?'

'Bless you, my sweetheart; thirty all told, counting Arthur and the Professor. Don't you worry about them. They're a grand bunch and very good about the household chores. Right now, they've taken themselves off to Poole to stock up for tonight's party.'

'What sort of party?' Lydia enquired.

'I suppose you could call it an end of term party. They've been ever so busy these past three months sorting out those wretched drug runners. Some of them will be off tomorrow and the rest on Monday, so Arthur was telling me. It's going to be very quiet. You are tripping over them one minute and wishing they were back the next. But tonight they're bringing Chris, Sophie and Juliet to join them.'

'Who are they?' This time, Sue was the questioner.

'They've been regular visitors here throughout the summer and a great help to Arthur. Sophie and Juliet are sisters; sixteen and nine. Chris is sixteen, too; he's a nice lad. But that's enough of that. You get yourselves sorted out and I'll do omelettes, chips and salad, if that's alright with you. Off you go now, close the front door when you've got your luggage, then up the stairs, turn right and go as far as you can. The bathroom's in front of you, my room is on the left and yours is on the right. I'll see you in the dining room in about twenty-five minutes.'

'Thank you so much, Mrs Cooper, you really are very kind. One last question – when do you expect them to get back?'

Mrs Cooper gave them a broad wink. 'Knowing them, we shan't see hide nor hair of them much before six o'clock. I know they're collecting the children sometime after five-thirty.'

It didn't take them long to unpack and after a quick shower they made their way downstairs and explored the public rooms. Three places had been set in the dining room, so they guessed Mrs Cooper would be joining them for lunch. 'She must feel rather outnumbered, with thirty men to cook and cater for,' Lydia remarked. 'I imagine the laundry bill must be hefty.'

Sue reassured her. 'The one thing they're not short of is money. I was in London when some of their treasures were auctioned at Christie's. The pieces were in terrific condition, all dating from the late fifth or early sixth centuries, and netted nearly seven hundred thousand pounds.' They wandered out into the garden and inspected the obstacle course. Lydia said it reminded her of a TV documentary about the award of a Green Beret to those recruits who wanted to become Commandos. 'They have to complete every part of the course within a fixed time; otherwise they aren't accepted and have to settle for some other form of military service. Apparently that applies to women as well.'

Just then, they heard the sound of a hand bell, and saw Mrs Cooper standing by one of the French windows. 'Lunch is served,' she called. 'I hope you've both good appetites.' They joined her in the dining room and were soon tucking in to tasty cheese and mushroom omelettes, crispy oven chips and a side salad, all washed down with chilled apple juice.

'What are your plans for this afternoon? Badbury Rings is worth a visit, and with the children still on holiday you're sure to find the ice cream van doing a steady trade in the car park, which is free, but the National Trust invite donations. If you still have time, you can drive over to Wimborne. It has a couple of tea rooms in the town centre and, of course, the Minster, which is very interesting, especially the clock with the quarter-jacks.'

'That's a great help, Mrs Cooper, and once we've done the washing up, we'll follow your suggestions,' Susanne replied. 'We're both thoroughly house-trained.'

'Don't you worry about the dishes. You've been on the road for most of the morning. Now how about some apple pie? I've warmed it up and there's vanilla ice cream to go with it.' Half an hour later, they were on their way and in no time at all they could see the clearly defined hill fort with a steady queue of cars turning off to take advantage of a popular tourist attraction on a fine summer afternoon.

'What shall we do, Lydia? Walk up to the main rampart and then go round, or cut across the centre to the north side? It's just turned two o'clock, so we've plenty of time.'

'Let's walk round when we get to the top. There must be some terrific views.' A well-marked path, largely ignored by the small children, brought them to the crown of the ancient earth-works. They made their way around the perimeter, taking note of the defensive ditches and wondering what it must have been like fifteen hundred years ago.

Susanne mused upon the likely scenario. 'We can't be sure what the area was like in Arthur's day, but it's likely to have been well-wooded. If Arthur was expecting the Saxon host to approach from the east or the south this would be a good place to see them, and have a force of cavalry lying in wait on the blind side of the hill to knock the stuffing out of the invading force just as they reached the first of the ramparts, while the foot soldiers defended the fort with the advantage of the ditches designed to slow the attack. At least that's what the children's guide to Badbury seems to think!'

'Sue, if Arthur asks you to stay, what will you do?' They strolled on and Sue gave a slight laugh. 'Good question. Obviously I'd be flattered, I can't deny it. Even so, I will say as tactfully as I can, thank you, Arthur, for paying me that compliment, but I'm afraid the answer is No.'

'Do you think he'll be angry?'

'I do hope not. Disappointed, yes – but if he is as wise and understanding as Merlin has given me to understand he won't be angry. In any case, I have a surprise in store for him which will come as quite a shock.'

'A surprise? What kind of surprise?'

'Dear Lydia, I want you to share that surprise when

it happens.' Sue stopped to look across to the north-east now that the sun was on the back of their necks: 'That way lies London.' She turned to the north-west: 'That way lies Gloucester, and it's my belief that underneath our feet is the chamber where Arthur and his men rested from their labours all those centuries ago. Call it female intuition, if you like. Anyway, I wonder what they've done with all that money?' She came out of her brief reverie. 'Did you say something about ice cream? Come on, we're more than half way round.'

There was a short queue but with two people at the counter, one handling the cornets and fillings and the other taking the money, they waited no more than a few minutes to be served. They sat on a grassy knoll watching the children roll down the steep banks. The sun was still hot and with nothing more than a light breeze, the kite-flyers had little success. Soon after three o'clock they left Badbury to the children and headed for Wimborne, and eventually found a car park on the north side of the town. It was a five minute walk to the town centre, where they made a bee-line for the Minster, grateful for its cool and quiet atmosphere. Compared with Dowdeswell Church, its proportions were closer to those of a cathedral.

The rest of the afternoon they wandered round the town, visiting the charity shops and finding a pretty tea room where they enjoyed a Dorset cream tea in the shady garden. When they returned to Kingston Lodge, there was clear evidence of occupation. Five gleaming jungle green Army Land Rovers displaying squadron markings and sporting short-wave radio aerials were parked in a neat row. Arthur was back in residence. As they approached the front entrance, they could hear laughter and the buzz of men's voices from inside the Lodge.

'What have we let ourselves in for, Lydia?' Sue straightened her shoulders. 'Well, in for a penny, in for a pound. Let's go, and it's your turn to ring the bell.' Lydia gave the bell pull a sharp tug and then stepped back to wait for one of the 'gentlemen' to answer the door. To her surprise, a girl of about her own age appeared as the door opened. She looked at Lydia and then at Susanne. The recognition was immediate, and she was back in the Great Room at Christie's auction house. 'You must be Guinevere,' then, turning to Lydia, 'I don't think we've met. My name's Sophie, and I've been asked to welcome you. Arthur will be so pleased to see you, and a little bit nervous as well. Would you like to follow me, please?'

She paused while they closed the door before leading them into the spacious sitting room. Sophie stood to one side as Susanne hesitated just inside the door with Lydia by her side. The men, who had been engaged in lively conversation, let out an involuntary gasp of surprise as they studied the young woman framed in the doorway and her companion. A young girl ran forward and gave Sue a brief curtsy. 'You're Guinevere, aren't you? My name is Juliet, and Sophie is my sister.'

'I'm very pleased to meet you, Juliet, and perhaps it's best if you call me Jennifer – Jennifer Cameliard. That is the name by which Merlin knows me, and this is my friend Lydia.'

'And what of Arthur?' The voice came from the far end of the room, and the men who had crowded forward to see the two young women stood aside as Arthur approached them and halted in front of Susanne, who sank down in a low curtsy. Arthur took both her hands in his, bowed his head and kissed them. When he raised his head again, he looked at her in admiration. 'You look just as I remember you when I begged your father for your hand in marriage. Never did I imagine that such beauty could survive the passage of the centuries. Welcome to the Lodge, our home for the time being, and welcome to my heart. But I forget my manners. Who is your graceful companion; does she have a name?'

'Arthur, she has done me a great favour in making this journey at my request. She is known to Merlin and now she is known to you. Her name is Lydia, and

I have known her since she was a baby. Lydia, may I present Arthur Pendragon?'

Arthur stepped forward, took Lydia's right hand, bowed and kissed it. 'From what kingdom do you come?' he enquired. Lydia glanced quickly at Susanne, who gave her an encouraging smile. 'Why sir, I live close to Gloucester, which in Roman times was called Glevum, not many miles from the Welsh border.'

'There's one guest you've still to meet, Lydia. Where's young Christopher? Let him greet our guests.' Christopher was ushered forward to add his welcome before drawing Sophie alongside. 'It was just three months ago on a lovely Sunday afternoon that Sophie and I came across a narrow entrance at Badbury, which led us into the heart of the fort. There we found Arthur and his company of knights.'

Susanne responded. 'I remember seeing you in London when you were at the auction house. At that time I was with my friend Lucy, but we spoke only to Merlin, at least Lucy did on that occasion. Where is he, by the way?' Arthur grunted. 'He muttered something about needing to speak to Mrs Cooper – and that reminds me, it must be time we took our places for supper.'

Before Arthur could say more, Susanne gave him her most winsome smile and said, 'I pray you will

214

excuse us for just a few minutes before we take our seats at the supper table. We both need to wear something other than a skirt and blouse.' Before he could protest, she had taken Lydia by the hand and hurried towards the stairs. Ten minutes later, they entered the dining room wearing more formal attire. Lydia was wearing a long black and silvered evening dress with thin shoulder straps and a blood-red gemstone in a silver setting suspended on a fine silver chain around her neck. Susanne wore a pale cream tussore silk ankle-length dress with the sea-green scarf fastened at her left shoulder with the turquoise clasp she'd worn at the BBC studio. Both girls looked stunning.

Arthur moved towards them. 'Come, ladies, you honour us with your presence. Therefore, you shall occupy the seats of honour. Lydia, you will be seated on my left, while Jennifer Cameliard, you take the Siege Perilous on my right.' While they waited for the food to be carried in, Susanne took the opportunity to study Arthur's friends. She wasn't quite sure what she expected, but what she observed took her by surprise. When she and Lydia had entered the sitting room, it was the men's clothing that caught her attention. They were dressed casually with open-necked shirts with a variety of check patterns and the cavalry twill trousers favoured by the county set. They could easily have been members of a country club, but the military vehicles outside marked them out as army officers. The second surprise was their height. Most of them were of middle height, perhaps 5'7" or 5'8" with no more than half a dozen near the 6'0" mark, of whom Arthur was one. As she looked around the table, she tried to guess which of them was Launcelot – Guinevere's lover and Arthur's closest friend.

'So what are you thinking, my sweet Guinevere?'

Nothing you would be pleased to hear, my lord, Susanne thought to herself. 'I was wondering how much or how little Merlin has told you about me. Has he spoken on the matter?'

'Only that he had warned you that Morgan le Fay is abroad and may do you harm and may make use of the many idle folk to stir up trouble for you. Is there more?'

'I think when the meal is over, we four – you, Merlin, Lydia and I – need to talk.' Arthur was about to reply when Merlin and Mrs Cooper, accompanied by the duty stewards, entered the dining room carrying great soup tureens and baskets of freshly baked rolls. Merlin took his seat at the other end of the table and said a short grace, 'May God bless us as we give thanks for all his gifts. Amen. A warm welcome to our honoured guests, Jennifer and Lydia.'

Lydia prevented Arthur from pursuing his exchange with Susanne when she asked if he could go round the table identifying the members of his company by name.

'I'm not sure you'll remember more than three or four when I've finished, but if I start with your side of the table, you've already made yourself known to Baudwin, then follows Bors, Carados, Tor, Cador, Tristram, Hector, Percival, Gawaine, Pelleas, Gareth, Launcelot, Kay…' While Arthur had been reeling off their names and pausing so that Lydia could register each one, Susanne stiffened as he named Launcelot, '… and finally Sagramore.'

Turning to Susanne, he said, 'You have been greeted by Agravaine and then follows Ywaine, Balin, Clariance, Bedivere, Bellinor, Brastias, Pellinore, Dinas, Lionel, Gaheris, Lamorak, Galahad …' This time, it was Lydia's turn to feel a wave of emotion as she looked upon the face of the youngest of Arthur's knights and Launcelot's son, '… and Geraint at the far end with Merlin and the children.'

The meal proceeded apace and at its conclusion, Merlin rose to address the gathering, 'Friends, our guests have been on the road for many hours and you will be on your way in the coming days to continue the work so well begun. It would be ungracious of us to keep the ladies from their beds, but there are matters for Arthur to raise with them. I would ask you to come forward and take your leave of them before we retire to the drawing room. Mrs Cooper will be glad of your help in clearing the supper table and laying it up for tomorrow's breakfast. On that note, I ask you to express thanks to her for the splendid provision she has set before us tonight.' A spontaneous burst of applause greeted the housekeeper as Juliet presented her with a bouquet of red and white roses. Arthur stood and one by one signalled his friends to come to the head of the table and take leave of Susanne and Lydia. In courtly fashion, both held out their right hand to be kissed, and as Launcelot bowed his head, Susanne felt colour flooding her cheeks. When Galahad came forward to Lydia, he gave her a broad wink and clasping her hand in his kissed her on her right cheek.

At Merlin's invitation Arthur and his two companions followed him into the drawing room. Four comfortable cushioned armchairs had been placed in a semi-circle around the unlit fire, the curtains were drawn and the door was closed.

'It rejoices my heart to have you both here,' Arthur began, 'and I hope you enjoy your visit, but courtesy demands that you share with us what has taken place in the months since Merlin first made contact with you some eight months before Christopher and Sophie guided him to our place of rest three months ago.' Arthur inclined his head towards Susanne, inviting her to speak.

'I'm sure Lydia joins me in thanking you for making us so welcome, which makes it all the more difficult for me to say what I have to say to be true to myself. I am not sure whether Merlin expected or wanted me to be here tonight, but in fairness to him I will try to explain my doubts. It is common knowledge that made headline news in the Press and on TV that I went missing in the Herefordshire Hills on the first Sunday in November last year and reappeared five days later in a confused and dazed state in Gloucester city centre.

'At that time, Merlin was making a country wide search to find you and your knights and it is more than likely that while he was in Cornwall he may have seen Morgan, who lives there earning a living as an artist in Clovelly. My guess is that he was careful not to be seen by her. When my disappearance was splashed on posters in the south-west – have you seen this woman? – both Merlin and Morgan headed towards the Herefordshire area because both of them recognised me as the striking image of your wife, Guinevere.' Susanne gave Merlin a long, searching look, which made him bow his head.

'I'm also inclined to think that Merlin backed a hunch and made straight for Arthur's Stone, where he found me in a deep sleep of total exhaustion.

But I am a fit young woman and there is no way I could possibly have slept for five nights and four days without waking up. Yet that is what I was led to think had happened, if it had not been for the fact that when I was given a thorough examination by the police surgeon she could find no sign of any injury whatsoever, or any bruises on my body and no reason why I should have slept for such a long time. During that time, I was visited by Merlin as if in a dream, and he drew attention to three imperatives of which I shall speak later.

'My belief is that I was not dreaming but being visited by Merlin and given drugs that kept me in a semi-conscious state while he continued to reinforce those imperatives. I think he camouflaged the burial space with brushwood so that I wouldn't be found until he was satisfied I had absorbed his instructions. I was to accept that my name was Jennifer Cameliard. But I also received three further directives: that you needed me and that I should keep that in mind at all times; secondly that I should be on guard against the plotting of Morgan, who would pursue me and do me harm; and the third was to set in hand some way of helping young people who were out of work to be given opportunity to do something useful with their lives before Morgan corrupted them. The term we use for this process is brain-washing.

'I last saw Merlin in November during a brief meeting at Stonehenge where his main concern was to gain information from my friend, Lucy, about how to find a buyer for your treasure. He made no further contact with me and I doubt that he was intending to do so.'

Arthur broke in at this point. 'What possesses you to say such a thing?'

Trembling slightly, but determined not to flinch at his tone of voice, Susanne replied firmly, 'Merlin knows that I am not Guinevere, but he saw me as someone who could divert Morgan away from you, so that I became the target of her bitterness and resentment. You should know, Arthur, that my name is Susanne Jennifer Mortimer; I am the twenty year old daughter of Doctor Robert Mortimer and his wife, Sarah. I am not your wife, my name is not Guinevere, but I felt I owed it to you to behave as if I were at this evening's supper, since I had no wish to embarrass you in the presence of your friends. You deserve better of me than that.

Furthermore, if it is within my power, I will do whatever I can to help you in your great undertaking to bind up the wounds that you observe in this country which in times past you did so much to protect. I feel sure you would rejoice to see what has been done in Gloucester, where a new Camelot offering hope to young men and women has been established as Merlin encouraged me to do.

But there is one thing more that both of you should know. Morgan has become a dear friend to me – an older sister who was deeply unhappy, but by the offer of friendship has found love and peace with a good man who cares for her. I believe it is time for you, her half-brother, and your counsellor, Merlin, to make peace with her, for she is more sinned against than sinning.'

Once again Arthur interrupted, 'How can you suggest such a thing?'

'You should be asking how could I not be asking such a thing. Consider, Arthur, these facts well known to you. How your father, Uther Pendragon, conspired with Merlin to seduce Igraine, the wife of Gorlois, Duke of Cornwall, into believing Uther to be her husband and to conceive his son in her womb. When Gorlois died a violent death soon after, Uther took Igraine to be his wife but as soon as she gave birth, the child was taken from her into Welsh exile for fifteen years.

'Have you ever considered what that sequence of events did to the child Morgan: her mother abused, her father dead by violent means, a step-father she had no cause to love and a mother grieving for her stolen child? How can I not urge you to make peace with Morgan? At my bidding, she is prepared to do as much – or am I to stand between you and cry 'Shame on you!'

'I have said my piece; I will say no more on the matter.' Then she turned to Merlin. 'I ask nothing of you, Merlin, except that you be as open and honest with me as I have been with you since we first met; then we can be friends indeed and in truth.

'Sirs, Lydia and I bid you goodnight. We will leave tomorrow after we have taken our breakfast. Just remember, Arthur, that I hold you in deep respect and affection. Goodnight, my lord.'

They left the room, leaving the two men to their thoughts.

Both girls were soon fast asleep and when the sunlight began to filter through the curtains the following morning, Susanne slipped quietly out of bed, had a quick shower, brushed her teeth and dressed in jeans and a white cotton tee-shirt. She crept downstairs and made her way to the kitchen where Mrs Cooper was busy preparing breakfast.

'Good morning, Mrs Cooper, isn't it a lovely day?'

'Oh my dear, I was going to bring you both a nice cup of tea in your room.'

'Lydia's still fast asleep and I have to get up once I am awake. I'll make tea for us when I get back; right now, I'm looking for Arthur.'

'He's gone for a stroll in the garden, just a few minutes ago. There's a garden seat in a shady little bower where he often goes when he has something on his mind. Just go out through the front entrance, turn left, then straight across the lawn – you can't miss it.' Sue didn't wait for any further information. 'Thank you, Mrs C. I'll be back soon to make tea.'

While most of the garden was given over to lawn, at one end there were clusters of bushes and a paved path inviting the curious to explore what lay beyond. She hurried across and the path led into a tiny glade with a rustic bench and a small rockery of alpine flowers and dwarf cacti. Arthur was sitting deep in thought, a reflective expression on his face, unaware of Sue's presence. She had almost decided to abandon her intention when she stumbled on a flagstone and gave an involuntary cry. Arthur looked up. 'Are you alright?'

'I'm fine. I was on my way to see you and then wondered if I should disturb you; you seemed lost to the world.'

'Why don't you come and sit down and tell me what gets you out of bed so early in the morning?' He stood up as she walked past the rockery and sat down.

He resumed his seat. 'You were saying …?' Sue drew a quick breath.

'Arthur, it was painful for me to say the words spoken last night and I could see the pain in your eyes. I would like to be more positive this morning. Before I fell asleep, I realised three things: the first concerns you and Morgan. I believe it might be easier for everyone if you could find time to visit Gloucester (Glevum as it used to be called in your day) and that when you meet Morgan I am there to act as a bridge between you. I care for Morgan and I know she trusts me. I also care for you and I hope you feel able to trust me to do whatever I can to reconcile you and your sister to one another.

'The second reason is that I really want you to see for yourself the work of the Camelot Centre which I named in your honour quite deliberately. You will see dozens of young people anxious to make something of themselves and be a credit to the communities in which they live. You'll also have the opportunity to meet the men and women who give freely of their time, skill and experience to help the young people succeed in their ambition. The support for the project has been amazing and I did it for you as much as for those youngsters.

'The third reason is personal. I would like us to spend time together and get to know one another. If

Merlin really expected me to fall into your arms the minute we met yesterday evening, he's not as wise as he may seem. I think he has a problem with women; perhaps the Nimue episode when he made a fool of himself was to blame. But leaving him aside, if you are prepared to spend a week or perhaps two weeks in Gloucester, we may discover whether we have a future together or be comrades in arms seeking the wellbeing of this country. What I cannot do is pretend to care about you from a sense of duty; that is not the basis for a true and lasting relationship. If my life is to be shared with yours it will be because I cannot contemplate life without you. The stakes are high and it will be interesting to see what my parents make of you!'

Arthur turned towards her. 'Perhaps I should call you by the name your parents use, if I am to meet them. Susanne, you have it in your power to knock a man down one day and lift him up the next. Yes, I admit that when I saw you enter the sitting room and assumed you to be Guinevere, I imagined we would be together again as man and wife. When you retired to your room, I had hard words to say to Merlin and he did not deny the truth of your claims and begs your forgiveness.

'Kingston Lodge has a well-stocked library and I picked up a book by a man called Hartley which

Merlin had suggested I might enjoy reading. One phrase caught my eye in his prologue: 'The past is a foreign country; they do things differently there.' These past three months have made his judgment undeniably true. My response, therefore, to your three proposals is a firm Yes on all counts. Merlin will be required to resume his duties in Oxford before very long and, apart from visiting my companions who are continuing to make life difficult for the drug runners I am at your disposal and will look forward to meeting Morgan, visiting the new Camelot and spending time with you. Now give me your arm and let us break our fast together.'

They walked slowly back to the house and there was a sense that an important watershed had been encountered, and a turning point in their relationship which drew a line under the harsh words of the previous evening and opened unknown yet exciting possibilities in the future.

'Heavens above,' exclaimed Susanne, 'I've forgotten all about Lydia's tea. I'll see you at the breakfast table.' She dashed into the house, made straight for the kitchen and a few minutes later was standing by Lydia's bed. 'Do you take sugar in your tea, Lydia, I've forgotten?' Lydia's face emerged from beneath the duvet. 'I had a dream that Galahad had asked me to marry him and I was just about to say

'Yes, please' when you spoilt it by asking about sugar in my tea!' Ten minutes later they had joined Arthur for breakfast. Nobody else was present and Susanne asked Arthur where they were.

'One squadron is making its way along the south-east coast towards Dover and the other is driving south-west towards Plymouth. We shan't be seeing them again until winter approaches and channel crossings in high powered launches are abandoned. Baudwin, Lamorak and I will stay here and at the beginning of November both squadrons will return and we will then have to decide what our next task will be.'

When they had finished breakfast, Susanne announced that she wanted to see Mrs Cooper to thank her for looking after them. Arthur stood up and said he would come out to see them on their way in a few minutes' time. Lydia hurried back to their room and re-emerged with their luggage while Susanne made her way to the kitchen, where she found Mrs Cooper enjoying a well-deserved cup of tea. 'I've just come to say goodbye and to say how grateful we are for all the kindness you have shown us since we arrived.'

'It's been a real treat to have you stay and even though you've been here less than twenty-four hours, I shall miss you both. I've made up a picnic box of sandwiches, fruit and bottled drinks for the journey home, and you must promise to come and see us again

228

but stay longer next time.' With that, she clasped Susanne in a warm hug. 'Mind you drive carefully – he's a good man and kind with it. I'm sure you know what I mean.' She turned away, her face flushed with emotion.

As the girls came out from the front entrance, they saw Arthur and Merlin standing beside Susanne's car. When Merlin began to walk towards them, Susanne wondered what was in his mind. 'Susanne, I have behaved shamefully towards you and I beg forgiveness of you. I will be as honest in my dealings with you in the days ahead as you have always been towards me since we met at Arthur's Stone. I wish you both a safe journey home to your families, and look forward to renewing our friendship. Fare well.' He bowed to them and made to return to the house, but not before Sue had taken him by the arm, 'Thank you, Merlin. All is well between us – may it remain so in the future.'

When Merlin had entered the house, the girls walked towards the car. Arthur asked Lydia if she would be kind enough to attend to the luggage while he had a brief word with Susanne. Taking her aside, he produced a small box. 'I may not claim you as my wife, but I ask you to wear this as a mark of the high regard I have for you and trust you will always think of me kindly.' Susanne opened the box and lifted out a gold rectangular ingot engraved on one side with a depiction of the sword Excalibur and on the other side the name Arthur. Taking it from her hand, he unfastened the clasp of the gold chain and placed it around her neck. 'At last night's supper, I seated you in a chair that would not normally be yours to occupy. Your proper place would have been on my left close to my heart. Merlin had already spoken to me of the courage, determination and grace you have displayed these nine months past. It seemed fitting, therefore, that you should sit in the Siege Perilous, the seat for those who have faced great danger, none more so than you, who faced my sworn enemy unflinching and now, as I discover, braver still in embracing her in true friendship. We will meet in Glevum and thanks to you bind up the wounds that have separated a sister from her brother.'

Arthur moved forward and wrapped his arms around her and then gently released her. As he did so, Susanne lifted her hands and drew his head towards her and kissed his lips. 'This is my gift to you, my lord.' Arthur stepped back a pace. 'Go safely on your way and God guard you till me meet again.' With Arthur's words ringing in her ears, the girls drove away, and as they left Kingston behind them Lydia said, 'May I ask you a question?'

'Of course you can.'

'Will you marry Arthur?'   Sue gave a contented

sigh. 'I don't know, but we haven't seen the last of one another. He'll be in Gloucester before long to be reconciled with Morgan, to visit Camelot and to spend time with me so that we can get to know one another properly. Why not ask me again when September has run its course?'

232

Epilogue

THE REUNION

At the end of September, Merlin prepared to resume his academic duties at Oxford. The house at Winterborne Kingston was closed up, leaving Arthur, Baudwin and Lamorak to head off to the east and contact Kay and the teams operating in Longship and Battleaxe. From their reports, it was evident that the drug runners were being given a hard time and the police had made a number of arrests in the Brighton area arising from the teams' intervention.

When they travelled to east Cornwall, they could see that Launcelot and his companions had a similar tale to tell, although finding access for Red Lion and Green Dragon had proved something of a problem with the inlets and beaches frequented by the drug smugglers. It had not been easy. Arthur gave notice that by the end of October they would call a halt to their patrols and rejoin Arthur at a location to be determined.

As Arthur and his two companions were driving north, after bidding their friends farewell, Lamorak remarked, 'Where next?'

'Why, Camelot, of course!'

'Camelot?'

'Well actually, I've booked us into a Ramada Hotel on the outskirts of Gloucester (we knew it as Glevum in the old days) and we'll be meeting two ladies of your acquaintance.'

'You mean ...?'

'Yes, Guinevere, or should I say Susanne, and my sister, Morgana, so that I can spend as much time as possible with the one and make my peace with the other.'

They arrived at the hotel and had time to shower and change before making their way to the dining room for the evening meal. Arthur gave some indication of the future programme. 'The English Channel can get very rough during the winter months and the cruisers being used by the drug runners may not be much in evidence. No doubt they'll look for other ways to stay in business. Meanwhile, I need to discover what other areas of concern we might turn our attention towards – no doubt Susanne will have some ideas in that direction. But for the moment, my apologies, gentlemen – you'll have to amuse yourselves tonight. I have a phone call to make.' He stood up and slapped his two friends on the back before striding towards the reception area to place a call to an Andoversford number.

A woman's voice responded, 'Glevum Lodge.'

'Good evening. Is that Mrs Mortimer?'

'Yes. Can I help you?'

'I hope so. May I speak to Susanne, please?'

'Who shall I say is calling?'

Arthur gave a chuckle. 'Just say, it's the Camelot King.'

Sarah Mortimer gave a small sniff. 'I'll call her. Susanne, there's a strange man on the phone wanting to speak to you. He calls himself the Camelot King.'

There was silence as Arthur waited, then a hardly suppressed snort of laughter as Susanne came on the line. 'My mother won't give me a moment's peace until I tell her who's called. Anyway, what can I do for you?'

'I'm booked in at a local hotel and I would like to see you.'

'This evening, you mean?'

'Yes. Is that a problem?'

'We've already had our evening meal. Where are

you ringing from?'

'I'm at the hotel but I can be at the intersection of Northgate and Eastgate in the city centre in about fifteen minutes' time.'

'I'll meet you at the intersection – don't go away!'

Susanne raced upstairs, gathered her purse and car keys, and paused long enough to place Arthur's gold ingot around her neck. On her way out of the house she let her parents know she was going out and not to wait up, and was gone as if the devil was chasing her. At eight o'clock she left her car in the parking zone and made her way to the intersection, where she had no difficulty in recognising Arthur despite the fading light.

There was a naturalness about their embrace which surprised neither of them, and if Susanne had harboured any misgivings in the weeks since they had last seen one another, they were swept away as they clung to each other. Not only did it feel right, but Susanne knew that it was right for them to be together.

They linked arms as they moved away in search of a friendly coffee-house, leaving two questions hanging on the evening air: who is Susanne Mortimer really? and what is the significance of the letters J.C. embroidered on a baby's shawl?

Coming Soon

The Badbury Tales
Book Three

MEN
OF
AVALON

By
Philip Elston

ISBN: 978-0-9565077-8-5

Reviews for

Return of the Raven

Wonderfully imaginative and vividly written. This is a splendid book suitable for children of all ages.
Michael Dobbs
Writer of *House of Cards*

Teenagers often get bad press where none is due and so it is heartening to read a story where ordinary young people are ready to put themselves on the line for the greater good. A mixture of legend and realism, *Return of the Raven* is a mystical adventure with its feet very much planted in the twenty-first century, but moving across the very real landscape of Southern England. It is an odd combination, but one which works as Philip Elston weaves a wonderful tale about the pressing problems of today's world that will renew faith in our youth's capacity for good.
Cristina George, Wiltshire

This book tells a splendid story, full of action and an impressive familiarity with today's soldiers and their business-like approach to problems, enhanced by the intervention of Arthur and Merlin – and the way they value the help of children.

John Haviland, Wiltshire

The author adopts a refreshing approach to Arthur, Merlin and the Knights of the Round Table. Arthur and his companions are awakened to life in the modern world using four-wheel drive vehicles as transport and their military skills to outwit today's criminals. The book wastes no time in engaging the reader's attention and many parents will enjoy reading it for themselves, while noting their children's eagerness to find out what happens next in Book 2 of the Badbury trilogy.

Warwick Turley, Devon

THE
KALAHARI
SERIES

FIVE BOOKS

ONE AMAZING STORY

WRITTEN BY AJ MARSHALL
PUBLISHED BY MPRESS BOOKS

The Osiris Revelations

THE BASTION PROSECUTOR

EPISODE 1

EPISODE 2

EPISODE 3

Rogue Command

AVAILABLE FROM SELECTED BOOKSHOPS
AND ONLINE

After ten years in the Royal Navy, Philip Elston read Theology at King's College London, where he also nurtured a keen interest in medieval history. Post ordination, he taught at secondary school level in Malawi and Surrey and later at a further education college in Leeds. His published work covers Central African & Commonwealth Studies, English Social History and a practical approach to personal issues with young people in mind. He has five grown-up children and lives with his wife near Salisbury in Wiltshire.

The Badbury Tales

Book One

RETURN

OF THE

RAVEN

ISBN: 978-0-9551886-8-8